I0549142

Oli's Gold

19th Century Frontier Survival

Book One

James Oliver Virmala

Edition 2

Cover Photo By Randy and Mary Smith

ISBN-13: 978-0-9972536-0-3

DEDICATION

This book is dedicated to my wife, Gloria, for believing in me and supporting my dream.

BOOKS BY THE AUTHOR

Oli's Gold Book One

Search For Oli's Gold Book Two

Return To Oli's Gold Book Three

To Be A Mountain Man

Trouble On The Kansas Plains

Frontier Justice

Return Of The Mountain Man

The Tall Man

The Prospector

The Green Valley

Twilight Of The Mountain Man

The Mother Lode

Quest Of The Mountain Man

CONTENTS

ACKNOWLEDGMENTS

I would like to thank my good friend Barb who supplied guidance and encouragement during the writing of my books.

Thanks to Mark who edits my books. I appreciate his historical knowledge which keeps me thinking and writing in the period of the book.

Thanks to the many friends who read the books and gave me feedback. Even more important sharing their favorite parts of the books which is priceless to me.

CHAPTER ONE

The soft ocean breeze ruffled the blond hair of the young man sitting on a coil of rope. His smiling blue eyes took in the activity as the ship *Gustav*, a three mast flute, was being loaded and readied to get underway. His broad shoulders and narrow waist were evidence of hard work in his 23 years.

The surroundings were a far cry from the small town he'd grown up in. The seaport was Helsinki, Finland, a Grand Duchy of Russia. It was 1838 and Helsinki boasted a theatre, university, and its own newspaper.

The young man, Olavi August, better known as Ōli, had traveled two days to the port from the family farm. His dream was to travel to America, where he could have a farm of his own.

"Good morning, young man!" Oli looked up at the round face of a stocky, white-haired seaman. "Will you be shipping out on the *Gustav*?"

Standing up quickly to shake the offered hand, Oli nodded. "My name is Oli August."

"You can call me Jolly. Grab your packs and let's go aboard."

Oli followed Jolly up the gangway. He gazed with excitement at the masts. Oli had signed up to work his way across the ocean as a ship's carpenter. He had worked two summers in a shipyard and had always enjoyed working and crafting wood.

One of his packs contained extra clothing, blankets, and necessary odds and ends. The other pack rattled with the sounds of his tools.

"This way, young man," Jolly said, leading Oli to the quarter deck.

Captain Jacob welcomed them, turning the log book towards them to sign in. Their signature, or mark, obligated them for the duration of the crossing. Alongside their name, they noted whether it was one way or round trip.

Oli turned to Jolly with surprise. "You're only going one way also?"

Jolly smiled. "Yes, I have business in the American West."

Pushing the log book back, Jolly added, "I'm a sail maker by trade, and this is my second cruise on the *Gustav*."

Captain Jacob laughed. "Jolly is always looking over the horizon for something better. He is a first-class sail maker, but no amount of my encouragement would convince him to make the return trip."

"Maybe he has a cute lass waiting in the West." Still chuckling, Captain Jacob walked away.

"Let's get below and claim our hammock space." Jolly crossed the deck to the starboard ladder.

Oli stood at the bottom of the ladder for a moment, allowing his eyes to get accustomed to the low light. The smell of new rope filled the space from the cargo areas of the deck below. The berthing deck was a large, open space, with hammocks suspended from the bulkhead to the center posts. The forward part of the deck was reserved for the head and galley. Oli smiled, hoping that the two wouldn't meet under heavy seas. There was a space for eating and lounging. There was also a locker for stowing the anchor ropes. Aft were compartments for the rope locker, and sail stowage.

"Tie your hammock to those two rings," Jolly said, pointing to the two next to his.

Awkwardly, Oli stared at the rings. "Jolly, one thing I don't have is a hammock. My hope was the ship supplied them."

"Not to worry," Jolly replied, "we will make you one up tomorrow, first thing."

Sitting against the bulkhead, Oli reached into his pack and withdrew a leather bound ledger. The 4 x 8 inch ledger was handcrafted and had a metal emblem riveted to the front.

His father had always told him that the best way to plan your future is to list your assets. Once you review your assets, the future is apparent. Taking the new wooden pencil from its holder, Oli carefully sharpened the point, letting the chips fall in his lap. Oli then listed the items in his packs and the clothes on his back:

Olavi August   1838, June 23

Personal Pack

2 wool shirts, 2 wool pants, 4 pair woolen socks, 2 long underwear, 1 pair boots, 1 darning needle, 1 leather awl, 1 knife, 1 razor, 2 wool blankets, 1 woolen coat, 1 woolen cap, 1 leather belt, 1 hammock from Jolly

Tool Pack

1 draw knife, 2 augers, 1 axe, 1 wooden maul, 1 chisel, 1 saw, 1 whetstone, 1 file, 1 roll of leather, 1 shaping plane and blades

Looking at the list, Oli felt confident that his start in America would be good. His father had worked in England for several years before returning to Finland and starting the farm. He had taught Oli to speak English. Reflecting on this, Oli opened the ledger again and added English to the list.

Oli looked up and watched Jolly come out of the galley. "Oli, I got us some biscuits and coffee from the cook."

Handing Oli the tin cup of hot, black liquid, Jolly sat down beside him. "I also got some honey for the biscuits. I put a bit in the coffee. The cook makes a mighty strong brew."

Oli sipped the coffee and smiled. "This is the first time I have had coffee, Jolly. We drank tea at home. I believe I could get to like this."

Oli continued to sip the hot brew while taking bites of the honey-covered biscuit. Taking the last drink of coffee and stuffing the remainder of the biscuit into his mouth, Jolly stood up and moved toward the ladder.

"Come along Oli. Grab your tools, and I will show you where the carpenter's locker is."

As they walked along the deck, Oli marveled at the coordinated movements of the crew. Everyone was busy securing the main deck in preparation to get underway later that night, at high tide. He felt a little like a square peg in a round hole. He wondered how long it would be before the ship's activities would become second nature.

Jolly opened a hatch near the bow. Oli looked in and saw the stacks of rough cut planks and beams. The strong smell of freshly cut wood surrounded him as he stepped in. The locker left very little room to move about. Most of the work would be done on the open deck. Oli thanked Jolly and turned to put his tool pack on a small shelf. He noticed the tie downs and secured the pack.

CHAPTER TWO

"Out of those canvas coffins. You're lying there like a bunch of landlubbers."

Oli looked up from his blankets. He saw the burly bosun walking through the berthing area. He stopped and looked down at Oli lying on the deck.

"Better get yourself a hammock, lad. You'll be a cripple in a week sleeping on a rolling deck."

Jolly swung out of his hammock and grasped the bosun's hand. Turning to Oli, he said, "This is Jon Erickson, the bosun. A better manager of the deck you will never see."

Pulling his socks on, Jolly assured the bosun that Oli would have a hammock before the end of the day.

Jon turned to Oli. "You came to this ship with good recommendations from the shipyard. I have a few things you can start on this morning. See me right after breakfast."

Oli smiled and nodded. At this time he was looking forward to something to eat. The *Gustav* had gotten underway shortly after 2 a.m., and Oli had helped handling the lines. It seemed like he had barely gotten to sleep before the bosun got them up.

After a quick stop in the head, Oli went to the galley. The cook had cornmeal mush and hot coffee. Oli noticed that the honey was missing from the coffee.

Oli stepped out onto the deck. He was momentarily blinded by the bright sunshine. The rolling of the ship knocked him off balance and he fell heavily against the railing mounted to the gunwale. He steadied himself with the help of the standing rigging. Oli looked in awe at the blue water and the billowing white square sails of the mainmast. He could taste the salt spray on his lips.

He heard Jolly laughing at him. "You'll get used to the motion soon enough."

Oli found the bosun and got a list of things that needed repair. The cook had also asked about getting two more shelves. Oli figured that if you take care of the cook, he will take care of your belly.

Working on the open deck, Oli closed his eyes briefly and listened to the sounds of the ship. The groan of the hull as it pitched through the waves, the snap of the sails; the creak of the lines as they strained; and the barking orders of the bosun along with the acknowledgements of the sailors.

Oli walked forward, swaying as the bow plunged through the waves. It threw up a fine spray over the ship. He noticed as he ran his hand along the rails that he could feel a coating of salt. Oli realized that he would have to take special care of his tools to prevent rusting. Here again, the cook would be good source of grease.

Oli's carpenter locker was near the foremast. He watched as two seamen climbed the rigging to adjust the sails.

Oli ended up with a fine hammock. Jolly knew his business when it came to working with canvas. Oli saw that Jolly laid on one blanket and was covered with another.

Jolly said, "The canvas hammock doesn't offer much warmth. You need a blanket on both sides to keep the chill off."

Oli was pleased to see Jolly had sewn a couple of pouches in the hammock, so smaller items could be stored. As he lay down to sleep the first night on the new hammock, he could smell the linseed preservative in the canvas.

The movement of the ship rocked the hammock, and Oli drifted to sleep with a smile and thought, *This is the life*.

The *Gustav* was bound for Boston. Talk of the need for construction workers there had made this Oli's destination. He figured that with his skills he could earn enough money to purchase his own farm within a couple of years.

Many emigrants from Finland had settled in Leominster, not far from Boston. This area had become available after hostilities had ended with the successful negotiations with Chief Sholan of the Nashaway tribes. Oli had heard that land was available, so he could grow vegetables or fruit.

The days passed quickly, and Oli was kept busy working on an endless list of items from the bosun. He took his turn standing watch, and enjoyed opportunities to climb the rigging and sit in the crow's nest.

As Oli looked from horizon to horizon, he realized just how small the *Gustav* was and how large the Atlantic Ocean was. He enjoyed seeing flying fish, and one day several whales went by, splashing the water with their powerful tails. Oli had a secret wish to be the first one on the ship to sight land.

Oli was finishing the repair of a forward hatch. The sun was hot on the deck and he had stripped to the waist. The muscles on his shoulders rippled as he lifted the hatch into place and secured the hinges. The hatch opened and closed smoothly. Oli smiled and turned, his blue eyes scanning the horizon.

"Still looking for America, are you?" Jolly asked. "It's time to get some chow."

Oli slipped his shirt on, and together he and Jolly headed for the galley. The sour-faced cook was filling plates with beans and a large biscuit.

Oli took his plate and sat down on one of the new benches he had built at the cook's request. As he bit into the biscuit, Oli smiled as he tasted the honey the cook had put in.

The *Gustav* was two weeks out of Boston when they hit a storm that would test the very souls of the crew.

Oli woke up feeling the shudder of the hull as it plunged through the waves. He rolled out of his hammock and grabbed his boots. Jolly was already leaving the galley with a slab of bread covered with a thick slice of cheese.

"No coffee this morning, Oli!" Jolly shouted over the noise of the storm. "Be a cold noon meal and supper too, unless this storm breaks."

Oli stuck his head into the galley. "Do you need anything, Cookie?"

"Yep, some calm seas and a dry firebox," the cook snorted.

Running up the ladder to the main deck, the wind almost took Oli's breath away. A wave washed over the deck, soaking him to the skin. Lines had been fastened on the main deck for the storm, and grabbing one was the only thing that prevented Oli from sliding across the deck.

Jolly shouted to Oli, "Get yourself some rain gear before you get too wet!"

"Too late!" Oli shouted back as he slid on some foul weather gear.

Oli's station during storms was assisting at the helm. While one seaman could handle the helm during fair weather, once the storm came up it was all two could do to hold the ship on course.

11

Captain Jacob stood by the helm shouting out course corrections. "You're doing a good job of holding her, boys. She's a fast-moving storm, so we may just make it out of this one yet."

Oli didn't know if he should take heart from the comment or be more concerned. The sharp snap of the mizzenmast rigging was followed by the crash and screams of men as the mast came down.

It went into the water on the starboard side, and was quickly pulling the ship around. If this continued, the *Gustav* would quickly be swamped and lost.

Grabbing his knife, Oli leaped to the rail and began to cut the rigging loose. Lightning flashed and he saw a terrified seaman clinging to the downed mast. Grabbing a line, Oli tossed one end to the man and wrapped the other end around a belaying pin. Wrapping his legs around the rail, Oli began to pull the man towards him.

Men around him were busy cutting loose the rigging. If they finished before the man was brought aboard, the seaman would be lost. A wave washed across Oli's back, almost tearing him loose from the rail.

Straining on the line, he felt the skin tear on his hands as the line slide through them. Suddenly, he was aware of someone next to him grabbing the line. Together, they pulled the man aboard and all collapsed on the deck as the mast broke free.

Oli looked up into the face of the bosun. "I thought we were going to lose both of you for a minute there. Good job, Oli!" He slapped Oli's shoulder and was gone.

The seaman stumbled by Oli and shouted, "Thank you, mate! I owe you!"

On shaky legs, Oli moved back to the helm. His fellow helmsman flashed a relieved smile as Oli grabbed his side of the helm.

They continued to fight the storm until mid-afternoon. What Oli did not realize was that they were fighting a hurricane with 75 mile-per-hour winds. They had contacted the hurricane as it was moving away from them, which shortened the length of the storm.

By 3:00 in the afternoon the winds had died down, but the seas remained heavy. Captain Jacob and the bosun were surveying the damage. The bosun looked at Oli at the helm.

With a smile on his face, the bosun said, "You will be earning your pay the next few days. We'll have to fix the structure as best we can. We will have to get a new mast once we make Boston."

Before he could answer, they moved quickly forward, checking the rest of the ship. Oli had wrapped rags around his hands. The salt water stung in the cuts from the line and even though his hands were work-hardened, fighting the helm had left him with blisters.

Captain Jacob came back to the bridge. "Oli, your hands look like hell. Go see the bosun and get something to put on them. You did a good job today, boy. Without your quick action, I would have been short an able-bodied seaman. The fellow has a wife and two youngsters back in Helsinki that will be beholden to you."

Feeling weak and a bit sick inside, Oli tried to smile and thank the captain. As Oli walked forward he felt for his knife. It was gone, no doubt lost while he was grabbing a line to throw to the seaman. The bosun gave him some grease with a minty smell to it. "It will burn a bit when you rub it in, but there ain't nothing better to start the healing of rope-barked hands. Now, go down to the galley and get a bite to eat. I heard Cookie got the stove lit. Then you can look me up and we will start fixing the damage. We checked the mast. It pulled clean and didn't poke no holes in the hull."

Oli thanked him and moved toward the galley. Several of the crew hunkered down near it. All were exhausted after fighting the storm for hours. As Oli walked up, they stood and congratulated him for his quick action.

A wiry, stoop-shouldered seaman walked up to Oli. Oli realized that it was the man he had tossed the line to. "My name is Matt Johnson, and I owe you me life."

Oli blushed a bit and said, "It was no more than anyone of the crew would have done, given the same situation."

"Maybe so," Matt replied, "but you were the one that was there and I'll figure a way to thank you."

Oli settled on a bench with a cup of hot coffee. *Hmm, honey,* he thought. Smiling, Oli picked up a thick cheese sandwich that the cook had put out and chewed it slowly, enjoying every bite.

It felt good to have the respect of the crew. Oli realized that it was not easily gained, nor easily kept, but for the moment it felt just fine.

It was early morning when the first ships' masts were sighted on the Boston Wharf. The storm was a distant memory and what could be fixed underway had been fixed.

Jolly and Oli sat on the forecastle and watched Boston emerge from behind the ships. To the port side, Oli could see a strip of land. He asked Jolly why they didn't land over there.

Jolly grinned. "That there strip of land is what makes Boston an ideal port. It protects the coast from the storms that come up from the south."

Jolly continued to tell Oli about the sound and the area, but Oli was too fascinated by all the ships and the city beyond to pay proper attention. He could see himself living and working in Boston, with the excitement of the wharf right outside his door.

"Hey, are you listening to me, Oli?" Jolly was pretending to frown. "I understand, Oli. I remember the last cruise. It was my first time in Boston. I spent the first two days just staring at all the wonders. Course, I spent the night drinking as much grog as they were willing to sell me and staring at the beauties."

At the sound of the bosun's whistle, both men fell to. Oli took his place at the windlass. It was time to make ready to drop anchor.

CHAPTER THREE

Jolly sat in the front of the whale boat, clutching his pack on his lap. Oli was just aft, sharing the seat with Matt Johnson. Matt would be returning with the *Gustav* after the mast was replaced.

"I still owe you, Oli," Matt said, staring straight ahead. He had a lost look on his face.

Before Oli could respond, Matt continued. "The return trip will be my last. When I went over with the mast, all I could think of is what would happen to my wife and children. When you threw me the line, I was so scared that it was difficult to let go of the mast and grab it. I was sure I would soon breathe my last."

Reaching into his pack, Matt withdrew a knife with a nine-inch blade and leather-bound handle. "I heard you lost your knife that night and I want you to have this one."

Taking the knife, Oli hefted it in his hand. "This is a fine knife, but I can't take it." Oli tried to return it.

Ignoring his hand, Matt continued. "It is fine tempered steel and is well-balanced if you want to throw it. No, it's yours, Oli, and a very small price to pay for my life."

The look on Matt's face convinced Oli that he should keep the knife. "Thank you, Matt. I will always think of you as a friend."

The whale boat bumped against the ladder leading up to the pier. Oli place the knife in his tool pack then, grabbing up both of his packs, he tossed them up to Jolly, who had already scrambled up to the pier.

Walking down the pier with Jolly, Oli bumped into him. "My goodness, Jolly, this pier is rocking worse than the ship!"

Jolly laughed. "You still have your sea legs. It'll take a bit to get your land legs back."

Stopping at the head of the pier, Oli gazed at the long brick warehouses. "My tools won't be much good here, Jolly. Not unless I can sharpen them enough to cut bricks."

He slapped Jolly on the back and they continued to walk toward the city.

"We'll turn left at the next corner," Jolly said. "I know of a boarding house where we can get a clean bed and decent food. And the price should not be too bad."

Oli reached into his pocket and fingered the coins he had received from Captain Jacob. Forty dollars was good pay for the crossing. Oli felt he may have gotten a bit extra for a job well done and his quick actions when the mast had gone over. Captain Jacob told him there would always be a berth on the *Gustav* if he ever wanted to return to Finland.

The boarding house was a long, two-story wood frame building. It had a full-length porch on the north side. It showed evidence of painting at one time, but it was now cracked and peeling. A chubby, rosy-cheeked lady met them on the porch. She wore a faded apron and had a scarf on her head that wasn't able to cover the rich brown hair.

"My sakes alive, if it isn't Jolly, back from the sea." Turning to Oli, she thrust out her hand. "I'm Sadie and this piece of heaven right here on earth belongs to me."

Accepting her hand, Oli smiled. "I'm Oli August, fresh in off the good ship *Gustav*. Jolly recommended your boarding house. I am hoping to find some work in Boston."

"You'll not have problems with that. There is a lot of building going on. I hear they still need carpenters at the Tremont House. It has indoor toilets, bellboys, even free soap."

Shaking her head, Sadie turned towards the door. "Let me show you to your room. Supper is at six sharp. If you're late, you'll have to wait till breakfast."

Jolly was right. The room, though small, was clean. They were sharing the same room. There were two single beds, one on each side of the room with a small table between them. There was a side board next to the door with a pitcher and bowl for washing up. A small window gave them a view of the street in front of the boarding house. Crisp, starched curtains covered the window. Oli and Jolly would store their packs under their beds. Supper was not a disappointment.

Sadie knew how to keep the boarders happy. The table was set with plates of roast beef, boiled potatoes, green beans, loaves of bread, and plenty of butter and gravy to top things off. There was cold buttermilk and plenty of hot coffee to wash things down.

Twelve guests, including Oli and Jolly, sat down to supper. When Oli thought he had eaten his fill, Sadie brought out two apple pies. Enjoying a slice of pie and his fourth cup of coffee, Oli turned to Jolly.

"You know, if I keep eating like this I will spend all my money buying bigger clothes." Laughing and joking, Oli and Jolly moved to the large porch.

The evening breezes were cool after a warm summer day. Oli leaned back with his eyes closed and thought, *Life in Boston is good.*

Sadie was right, there was lots of work for a carpenter. Jolly had heard that Uno Maki was working on the Tremont. Uno was a short, barrel-chested man. His forearms would rival many a man's calf. Uno's thick, rough hands had laid many a brick. Jolly was assigned to help with the digging of the trench for the running water.

Uno looked at Oli. "Do heights bother you?"

"Not a bit," Oli responded.

"Good, follow me." Uno led Oli to a job they were working on up the street. "The slate roof is leaking. We need to go up and tar the valley area."

Nodding, Oli looked around for a way to climb up to the roof. Uno motioned Oli to follow him.

"Let's build a fire to melt the tar first. The stuff is around the side of the building."

Oli followed Uno Maki's lead and found the bucket, blocks of tar, and a narrow paddle for smearing on the tar. A grappling hook with a length of line lay nearby.

Oli collected some loose pieces of wood lying around to build a fire and quickly had the bucket full of bubbling tar.

Uno picked up the hook and line. Walking to the front of the building, he swung the grappling hook in a wide arc and sent it flying to the roof. The hook clanged and clattered on the roof. A firm jerk of the line told Uno that it had hooked.

Oli stepped forward to grab the line, but Uno put his hand up to stop him. With hat in hand, Uno said a quick prayer.

He turned to Oli. "'Tis always a good idea to say a prayer before climbing. First, you pray for a secure hook on the roof. Then a quick prayer for the one that climbs, in case the hook isn't as secure as we hoped."

With a forced smile, Oli grabbed the line. "I have great faith in your arm and accuracy." Nodding briefly to pray, Oli climbed hand-over-hand to the roof.

The days of summer flew by, and Oli was never without work. Before he knew it, fall was in the air. Oli and Jolly sat on the front porch, smoking cigars and sipping wild berry brandy.

Enjoying the warm, sweet liquid running down his throat, Oli turned to Jolly. "So when do you plan to continue on the business in the West?"

Jolly sighed deeply. "I hear there are wagon trains leaving from St. Louis in the spring. I hope to be on one of those trains."

Shaking his head, Oli replied, "Jolly, we have it good here. We work every day. We are saving money. I plan to get a farm in a couple years. We could work it together, partners."

Jolly smiled. "What I have in the West is rich. Maybe when I come back I will buy us both a farm. We'll hire workers and sit on the porch and enjoy cigars and brandy all day long."

Oli laughed, slapping his knee. "That would be a great life, Jolly. But if a man sits around too long he gets fat and soft. No, Jolly, you can keep the riches. I'll work for what I get. Of course, you will always be welcome on my farm to help pick vegetables and milk the cows."

Adjusting his chair and pouring a bit more brandy into each of their glasses, Jolly reflected.

"You are right, Oli. No one gets rich without working. Maybe my trip west will be a long ride out and a long walk back, but I have to follow this up just to satisfy my curiosity."

They then sat quietly, chairs tilted back, their feet on the rail, each with their own thoughts while watching the horses and buggies go by.

* * *

Winter came early and hard to Boston. Construction came to an abrupt stop, leaving the laborers to survive on their meager savings, or leave the city and head for logging camps to the north. The weather had been cold and snowy, with one nor'easter after another coming through.

Each morning, Oli and Jolly would leave the boarding house, each carrying a shove and an ax. They would compete with others shoveling roofs and walks, or removing ice with the ax or splitting wood. Many days they came home with pockets as empty as their stomachs.

Just after the holidays, Sadie had learned the name of a man that was hiring for snow removal in the city. Fortunately, there had been a lot of snow to remove and Oli and Jolly managed to get onto the crew. The pay was low, and only as regular as the storms, but it would get them through the winter.

It was mid-winter in 1839, and Sadie was serving stacks of pancakes with dark maple syrup. Oli had learned the boarding house reach well and quickly dragged three thick pancakes onto his plate. He was spreading butter and pouring syrup on the stack when Sadie announced that it would be nice if someone caught some fish for supper.

"You know, Jolly, I bet we could do quite well off the main pier," Oli concluded. "We haven't been fishing since November. Fresh fish would be tasty."

Jolly looked out the window. "You're right, Oli. The sun is out and the wind is calm. After we eat, we can grab our poles and try our luck. That is, if Sadie can come up with some bait."

"Don't you worry," Sadie chimed, "I've got some bait."

As they left the boarding house, the bright sunshine reflecting off the snow blinded the two men for a moment. With fishing poles in hand, they walked briskly to the pier, keeping an eye out for icy patches. Soon, they were settled down to do some serious fishing.

Pulling his collar a bit higher, Oli looked over at Jolly. "Are you getting any bites?"

"Not a one," Jolly scoffed. "I am going up the pier a ways."

Oli was busy jigging his pole when he heard a cry. He looked over. Jolly was gone! Oli ran towards where Jolly had walked. His feet hit a sheet of ice and it was all he could do to stop from going over the side of the pier. There was Jolly floundering in the frigid water.

Oli hurried down a nearby ladder. "Jolly! Jolly! Swim this way and I'll grab you!"

Struggling, Jolly was able to get closer to Oli. Grabbing his collar, Oli lifted Jolly from the water and dragged him onto the pier.

"Damn clumsy fool," Jolly muttered through chattering teeth. "I slipped on the ice while sitting down and the next thing I knew, I was in the water."

Oli wrapped his coat around Jolly, and the two, half walking and half running, headed back for the boarding house. Sadie rushed into the room after hearing Oli's shout.

"My God! What happened? Get those wet clothes off and stand near the stove. I'll get some blankets."

Sadie ran from the room and was back quickly with blankets and a bottle of Scotch under her arm. "You'll need more than blankets to warm those old bones, Jolly."

Sitting next to the potbelly stove, Jolly sipped the Scotch, still shivering. Oli stood there, slowly warming up. He had not noticed the cold when they were running from the pier, but once in the house the chill hit him.

Looking at Oli's worried face, Jolly smiled. "Don't you fret about me. I have been far colder on some North Atlantic crossings."

Morning came with bright sunshine sparkling on the snow. Frost was making its exotic patterns on the windows. Oli sat in the dining room, sipping hot, strong coffee. It was a double sugar morning. He heard Jolly moving around slowly in the room above. Jolly limped down the stairs and came to the table.

"I'm stiffer than normal this morning. One of the things about getting old is your bones remind you of your age regularly." Jolly sat heavily. "If you don't mind, I will go back to bed after breakfast. I didn't sleep too good last night, and don't feel like facing the cold outside this morning."

Oli stared at his friend. "Jolly, you get your rest. I'll ask Sadie to make you a good hot soup. That will get your bones limbered up."

With breakfast over, Oli left the boarding house and headed for the snow removal gang. He was concerned. He had never seen a day that Jolly didn't step lively and enjoy the prospect of a good days work.

They were shoveling the snow into a large sled pulled by two Holstein oxen. After the sled was loaded with snow they emptied it into the bay. This was repeated for ten hours each day until the latest storm had been cleaned up.

It was getting dark when Oli walked hurriedly toward the boarding house. Shoveling all day was exhausting. Maybe he should work in a logging camp next winter, Oli thought. Many of the homes and buildings burnt coal, and on a cold day with a down draft the smoke lingered around the streets. The air in the woods would be fresher.

Oli was keeping his mind working so he would not worry as much about Jolly. Hurrying into the boarding house Oli pushed the door shut with his foot and pulled his mittens and coat off.

Sadie was sitting in the dining room staring into a half empty cup of coffee. Looking up, Sadie moved to a pot of coffee sitting on the potbelly stove. She poured a cup for Oli and they sat down facing each other.

"Bad news, Oli." There were lines of worry on her face. "Jolly is running a fever. I have been encouraging him to eat hot soup, but his appetite is not good."

"Maybe a hot cup of tea with honey might help," Oli offered.

Sadie brewed the tea and Oli went to the room with a steaming cup. Jolly was sitting up in bed. He coughed hoarsely and wiped his mouth with the back of his hand. "I feel like a damn baby with all of you waiting on me. I will be better tomorrow, you'll see."

Oli set the tea on the table next to Jolly. "You drink this, Jolly. It will help get your blood flowing and you will be up in no time."

Sitting on his own bed, Oli leaned back and put his hands behind his head. Jolly propped himself up with one elbow and took the cup of tea.

"We need to talk, Oli."

Looking at Jolly, Oli shook his head. "You just need to rest right now. We will have plenty of time to talk in the future."

Jolly sipped the hot tea and looked thoughtfully at the window. A sudden series of coughs racked Jolly and his head fell back on the pillow. "No, Oli, now is the time."

He paused before he continued. "Some years back, I was traveling in Spain. I stayed with a family working in their vineyard for the summer. I talked of sailing back and forth from America. One of the workers, an old Spanish gentleman, and I became good friends. When fall came I was ready to move on and he called me over.

"He said he was the last one alive in his family. The family had been given a map years before showing an area in the American West. One of his great uncles had served in the Spanish army in Mexico. He and other soldiers were transporting gold back to Mexico City from far up along the mountains when they were attacked by Indians. All but his uncle were killed. The stock was stolen or killed. He had survived more by luck than skill. The soldiers had hidden the gold before they had been defeated. Prior to leaving, his great uncle drew a map so someone could come back for the gold.

"He became ill on the trek back to Mexico City and ended up back in Spain with the map. Knowing that no one would understand why he did not turn the map over to his superiors, he just kept it. It had been passed down in the family. The old Spanish gentleman offered the map to me. He knew that he would never get to America. He had no family to give it to. I guess I became his family."

Jolly coughed several times before continuing. "If I do not get well, I want you to have the map, Oli. And mind you, I intend to get better."

Oli stared at a crack in the plaster wall. "Jolly, I don't like this kind of talk. You know you will be getting better and what you have told me was not necessary."

Both men lay in the room staring into the dark. The tea seemed to help Jolly's cough. They were not as hard or as frequent.

Oli was beginning to doze off when he heard Jolly say. "It's sewn into a pouch in my pack, just in case."

The next few weeks seem to drag by. Jolly would get a bit better and then have a relapse. Oli was hoping the warmer breezes of spring would help. The doctor said Jolly had pneumonia. He said that Jolly was a strong man to have fought back so many times.

Oli was sitting next to Jolly in late March. Jolly's fever was up again and he was going in and out of delirium. Oli was keeping cold compresses on his forehead.

Suddenly, Jolly looked him in the eye and with a raspy voice he said, "My friend, the gold is yours."

Closing his eyes, Jolly's breathing became more shallow, and then stopped. Oli sat there, his throat aching. Tears spilled out of his blue eyes.

There was a soft knock on the door. "Will you be coming down to breakfast, or do you want me to bring something up?"

Oli turned to the door. "Come in, Sadie. He is gone, his fight is over." Oli heard a stifled cry and Sadie slowly came in the room.

"You know," Oli said sadly, "I didn't even know Jolly's last name. He was my best friend and I never asked him once." Oli and Sadie held each other and wept with silent tears over the loss of a true friend.

CHAPTER FOUR

Oli buried Jolly in a quiet ceremony. Just he and Sadie were there to pray over him. Using what money Jolly had accumulated, Oli had paid Sadie, the doctor, and the undertaker. He bought a fitting headstone so those walking by in the future would know Jolly had had a friend.

Oli could not stay at the boarding house after Jolly died. With the money that was left from Jolly and the money he had saved, he had $78. The dream of owning a farm felt very far away. Sitting alone in the dark bedroom, Oli made his decision. If he wasn't going to be able to follow his dream, he might as well start out by following Jolly's dream.

Oli gave Jolly's personal things to Sadie, but kept the pack containing the map. Uno had admired his tools in the past. Oli did not see a need for them on the trip west. Uno gave Oli a fine knee-length deerskin coat in exchange for his tools.

He said his goodbyes to Uno Maki and Sadie. Hefting his packs, Oli started walking west. Uno had been to Buffalo, New York, before and recommended Oli go to Albany and ride the barges on the Erie Canal. Albany was a little over 100 miles west of Boston. Oli figured it would take about a week.

The first night, Oli found a quiet spot near a creek. Once he had eaten a light meal of hard bread and smoked fish, he made a small fire to brew his evening coffee. Oli reflected on his choice of coffee rather than tea. While he still enjoyed tea, when he sat with a steaming cup of coffee the aroma and bold taste was much more comforting.

Removing the map from Jolly's pack, he studied it while sipping the brew. The map was engraved on a piece of leather about 18 inches round. The map showed a line of mountains, a river, a jagged crescent, three crosses, and several markings leading towards Mexico City.

There were markings showing distance, ending at a dot near the three crosses at the edge of the mountains. Oli finally figured that these distances were measured in days walking. He now knew why Jolly talked of going west. The mountains had to be the Rocky Mountains.

Oli carefully sewed the map under the lining of the deerskin coat. He moved out just as the sun was coming up. Frost on the ground crunched under his boots. The sun felt warm on his back. This was the favorite time of year for Oli. Winter was gone, trees were budding, and early flowers like crocuses were blooming. He would close his eyes for a moment and listen to the chipmunks and birds welcoming the day.

Once in Albany, Oli set up a camp near the fork of the Hudson and Mohawk Rivers. Collecting some twigs and dry grass for tinder, Oli struck a piece of flint with his knife, sending a shower of sparks into the tinder. A wisp of smoke came up, which he blew on softly to encourage it to burst into flame. Once he had the fire going, he set a pot of water to heat.

The air temperature was around 50 degrees, but it had been going below freezing at night. Earlier that day, he had walked into town. Oli had picked up a few carrots and a nice potato. He had a bit of smoked fish left and planned to make a hearty fish soup.

While the water was heating, Oli took out his and Jolly's hammocks. With one he fashioned a tent and the other he used for a ground tarp. Under the ground tarp, he made a bed of balsam branches. Stepping back, Oli looked around his modest camp. He felt quite at home. It was time to sit down with his ledger and evaluate what his assets were:

1 wool shirt, 1 wool pants, 2 pair woolen socks, 2 long underwear, 1 pair boots, 1 darning needle, 1 leather awl, 1 whetstone, 1 knife, 1 razor, 6 fish hooks, 1 roll of leather, 1 blanket, 1 deerskin coat, light duty rope, 1 woolen cap, 1 ground tarp, 1 tent, 2 flints, food for 3 days, 1 coffee pot, 1 cook pot, 1 belt, 1 mess kit (cup, plate, bowl, spoon)

Looking at the list, he felt that he was in good shape to start the trip with only a few needs. He still had $73 in his money belt, which was an asset, but he dared not list that. Prior to booking passage on the canal, Oli added one shirt, one pair of pants and his socks. He figured that his underwear were just fine. They were a bit thinner due to age, but perfect for summer wearing. The knife he had received from the grateful Matt was now sported in a sheath on his belt. He purchased a good amount of hard bread and beef jerky. It was time to move on.

* * *

An early morning mist was rising from the Erie Canal. The mules on the tow path were straining to pull the barge out of the lock in Durhamville. The Erie Canal had opened just over 10 years before, and ran 363 miles from the Hudson River near Albany to Lake Erie at Buffalo.

Oli was enjoying watching the hoggee, or driver, handle the team as they moved forward. He was leaning against a bale of goods and chewing on a piece of beef jerky. The jerky was a far cry from the breakfasts Sadie would make. Oli stood up on the barge and stretched.

The canal was 40 feet wide and four feet deep. The maximum lift of a lock was 12 feet. Lake Erie was 600 feet higher than the Hudson River. It took

50 locks to make the trip. He had heard talk that they were making the canal bigger. He shook his head, it didn't make sense. From what he saw, it was plenty big.

The towpath ran on only one side of the canal; therefore, the path had to be shared. Oli watched the hoggee stop the team and sink lines into the water. The oncoming barge moved past them, with the mules stepping over the line as they proceeded to the lock. Once the other barge passed, the hoggee started their mules again. The act was repeated over and over again during the trip.

Oli's plan was to find and join a group heading west from Buffalo, then work his way down to St. Louis. There he could join a wagon train and go west. Even though most wagon trains organized in Independence, Missouri, Oli had heard some could be found in St. Louis.

He met two brothers on the barge who were heading to St. Louis. Tom and Isaac Franklin were about Oli's age, and heading west to become buffalo hunters or trappers. They had not decided which, but knew either would be wild and exciting.

Tom was about six feet tall and thin. He had a firm, square jaw and light brown hair. Isaac, whom they said took after his mother, was shorter and had a round face and blond hair. He carried a bit more weight than his brother Tom, but Oli figured that much of that weight was muscle.

The brothers had made arrangements to journey down to the Ohio River, and then on to the

Mississippi and up to St. Louis. They told Oli that they were sure that there would be room for another man on the trip.

Both of the boys proudly sported Kentucky long rifles. They hadn't had the flint lock changed to percussion cap because their plan was to get some Hawken rifles when they got to St. Louis. The larger caliber Hawken rifles were more popular with mountain men.

Oli enjoyed their company and listened to the excitement in their voices as they talked of the adventure. Oli didn't have a gun, and figured all he needed for the time being was his knife. When he got to St. Louis he would decide what else he needed.

The excitement of Buffalo was short-lived. The three men left the rough and tumble wharf nightlife a few dollars poorer, but smiling over the memories.

Oli and the Franklin brothers met up with the group headed for boats going down the Ohio River. They carried goods from New York and Pennsylvania to sell in St. Louis. They would then make the trip back with furs.

The boats were about 30 feet long, with flat bottoms and high, thick sides to offer protection from any attacks. There were two openings on each side for oars. They would be necessary when the boats returned upriver. Going downriver, they would be using push poles and the benefit of the current.

Henry Wilson was the top boss of the outfit. He had four boats and was happy to have another hand.

Looking Oli over, Henry asked, "You got a gun hidden in one of the packs?"

"No, I got no gun, but do have a knife," Oli proudly responded.

"Well, if we run into any hostiles on the trip down, we'll have to see what that there blade will do against arrows." Henry turned and spit a stream of tobacco juice.

Turning back, he smiled. "You can load guns can't you?"

"That I can do, I learned to load and shoot in the army."

Oli picked up his packs and followed Henry to the boats. Tom and Isaac were in the same boat as Oli. They had already stowed their gear.

The boss of the boat pointed to an area in the bow. "Set your packs up there. You'll be starting with a pole on the port side. I'm Boss Tuck, if you need anything."

Oli smiled and began to introduce himself, but Boss Tuck had already walked away.

The river was swollen from the spring thaw. The muddy torrent had plenty of branches and a few logs floating in it. As Oli climbed aboard, he saw what resembled a small island float by.

"What the heck was that?" a startled Isaac said to no one in particular.

"Let me help you with that," Tom said. "The character sitting on the cargo is Frenchy. He's been going downriver with Henry Wilson for two years."

"So you be Oli, hey?" Frenchy said, looking Oli up and down. "It looks like we will be earning our keep this trip. After the bosses finish their meeting, we will be shoving off. They will handle the rudders."

"We have to keep the boat going a bit faster than the current, so he can control the direction. If we float at the same speed as the current, the rudder is of no use. We'll be using our poles for moving the boats forward and assisting with changing direction."

"Keep your attention on the boat boss. He will keep his attention on our course and, with luck, keep us out of trouble."

Boss Tuck came back to the boat. He pretty much repeated what Frenchy had said and then added, "Boss Henry will be in the lead boat, we will be the last boat. It is spring, and some of the Indians are looking for a little excitement to shake the kinks out of their muscles after a long winter. So you all stay sharp and we will have a good trip."

Each boat was manned by five men, with the boss on the rudder and two pole men on each side of the boat. The goal was to keep the boats bunched up for safety. With the swollen river, that was a challenge.

Late morning the first day, a cold drizzle started. Boss Tuck broke out rain slickers for everyone and they kept right on heading downstream. Noonday stops were brief. Boss Henry would find an acceptable spot to pull in, and the boats would raft together. Someone would get a fire going for coffee. Then everyone would scatter into the brush to take care of personal duties.

The meal consisted of biscuits from breakfast and any leftovers from supper the night before. If there weren't any leftovers, jerky or cheese was always available. The day would end about an hour before sunset.

A wiry Spanish fellow on the number two boat was the cook. He sported a long, tobacco-stained beard. Supper consisted of hot biscuits, beans, strong coffee, and anything the boats had managed to catch or kill during the day.

Everyone pitched in to help Jose get set up: Hauling his cook box off the boat, collecting enough wood for evening and morning, and setting up a fly tarp if there was rain. Each man was responsible for his own dishes.

Oli grabbed an axe and headed out to get some more wood. He heard Isaac call behind him. "Watch out where you step in those bushes."

Breakfast was more beans, biscuits, and lots of hot coffee. Once in a while, Jose would drag out a big cast iron pan and make pancakes. They would pour molasses on them.

It took six days before the boats traveled the tributary and entered the Ohio River. This would lead them to the Mississippi River and then on up to St. Louis. The Ohio River was also flooded from the spring thaw, with many areas overflowing its banks.

Because of the additional width, its current appeared much slower. Rapids could quickly spread the boats apart. Boss Henry called them all together after supper the first night on the Ohio.

"We have had a good trip so far. It was more difficult to attack on narrow, swift water. Here on the Ohio, we will make a much easier target. I want all the boats to keep their guns loaded. Two men will be on the poles while the other two keep watch. Noon meals will be eaten on the water. We need to stay in the center as much as possible."

"The next 100 miles is the most dangerous. When we get through this stretch we will take a couple days to rest up. There is a small landing with a decent watering hole, even a few working ladies."

There wasn't much talk that night. Everyone sat around the fire. Most were busy oiling and cleaning their firearms.

Isaac sat next to Oli. "You and I are on opposite watches. You can use my rifle when you're on watch."

"I appreciate that, Isaac. I now think I may have made a mistake not picking up a rifle in Buffalo," Oli commented while he poked at the fire with a stick.

He was worried. Boss Henry wasn't the type of man to create fear unnecessarily. Oli was sure there was a real concern on Boss Henry's part. They had passed a boat going up the Ohio earlier in the day and Oli was sure that Boss Henry had received a warning during the brief visit.

Tom came up beside Oli while he was cleaning his dishes in the river. "We got the first watch. Boss Tuck said we rotate every hour to keep everyone alert."

Oli finished up his dishes and sat back on the bank. "Your brother told me I could use his rifle for my watch. I did see Boss Henry open a box of guns this morning. I think his intentions are to have extra rifles in each boat."

Tom turned and headed back to the fire to get one last cup of morning coffee. Oli watched him walk away. Tom was a tall man. When he walked, he stepped noiselessly with an even, smooth gait. Oli smiled and thought, *they're will be a good mountain man.* Oli stood as tall as he could and tried to mimic Tom's walk. He felt he had the walk, but he was sure the uneasy feeling in his stomach about the next few days was not shared by Tom.

"Hey Oli!" Boss Tuck hollered, "Go up to Boss Henry's boat and get us four rifles. I told him I had me a first-class loader on the boat, so we get two extras."

Laughing, Oli jogged towards the lead boat. "Boss Henry, I was sent to get the extra rifles for the number four boat."

Henry pulled four rifles from a crate and leaned them against a tree next to the boat. He then handed Oli a possible bag filled with powder, caps, patches, and balls. "Your boat has the most important position, Oli. I don't want to scare you, but if we are attacked, it is the last boat they go for."

41

"Don't worry, boss," Oli said as he slung the bag over his shoulder and collected the rifles, "we won't let you down. If we're attacked, we'll do our share."

"I know you will. I only hire men I can depend on. I know you didn't show up with a gun, but I have a great deal of respect for men who have been in the army. Tom let me know about your past even before you mentioned it. That's why you are on boat number four. That's where I put the best men."

Oli headed back to his boat with his head in the clouds and feeling the weight of the four rifles. They were French-made rifles fitted with percussion caps. The barrels were shorter than the Kentucky long rifles Tom and Isaac had.

Once on the boat, Oli inspected each rifle for good operation. He then loaded them and placed the rifles strategically around the boat for quick availability.

For two days the boats proceeded downriver without incident. With everyone on heightened alert throughout the day, it was difficult to turn off and sleep at night. Four hour watches were set up, with some men on the boats and others on the perimeter.

The cook fire was kept low, and Boss Henry cautioned everyone about staring into the fire. It would create brief night blindness, which could be deadly in the event of an attack.

A pot of coffee was kept next to the coals, and by the middle of the night Oli was sure that his mess spoon would stand in it. Though it was strong enough to cut with a knife, Oli appreciated its eye-opening effects. Jose always had biscuits in his cook box, and from somewhere he came up with some tins of jam.

Just after pushing out to the middle of the river on the third day, some arrows came flying in. Most struck the water, but two stuck in the cargo packs on boats two and three. Everyone ducked down behind the sides of the boat, searching the shore for any sign of the hostiles.

It was evident that they had no intention of doing anything more than harassing the boats. Heart pounding, Oli looked over the edge.

He heard Frenchy come up beside him. "Settle back, Oli. They didn't even put a canoe in the water. Tomorrow, we have some rapids to navigate. If we get spread out, that is a place to worry about."

"How do you live with the worry, knowing an attack is coming?" Oli asked, sitting back against the side of the boat.

Frenchy put a plug of tobacco into his cheek and offered Oli a chew. Oli declined, but thanked him for the offer. After a couple chews, Frenchy spit over the side and took a long look at Oli.

"The fear you feel is what will keep you alive. You recognize your own mortality, so your senses will be at their best. When an attack comes, people do one of two things: They freeze or react. If one freezes, often by the time you react it is too late. The other sees the danger, and will be planning while reacting. He does not stop to think about his own life, but goes into action."

"I just watched you when the arrows came in. I saw no hesitation on your part. You were alert and ready for whatever came." Frenchy spit again and nodded. "Yep, you reacted. Now, we need to react and get on them poles."

Taking one more look toward the shore, Oli moved to the port side and lifted up the pole.

Everyone was a bit more cheerful that night at supper. The incoming arrows had broken the tension. Tom and a man from boat number two were arm wrestling. Frenchy and Jose were sitting on a log, holding a spitting contest.

Jose leaned back and smiled. "By golly, Frenchy, I think I got you by a good twelve inches."

Frenchy scoffed. "Just wait until I get this chaw worked up. I'll pass you by another twelve inches."

Oli walked to the edge of the water, enjoying listening to the banter between Frenchy and Jose. He looked around the camp. The watches were set. Four men who had a later watch were sitting on a blanket and playing poker. It was low stakes poker. Boss Henry wouldn't have allowed anything else on a trip. A man loses too much money, and the next thing you know you have trouble.

Oli noticed Isaac sitting upstream just a bit. Walking over, Oli asked, "What time is your watch?" Oli already knew what time Isaac's watch was, but unlike the rest of the crew, Isaac looked rather sullen.

"I have the early morning watch, Oli." Shifting to face Oli, Isaac continued. "I was real scared when the arrows came in. I saw everyone ready, I was ready, but I was praying as hard as I could that the Indians wouldn't continue attacking. I was afraid I might wet myself."

"Don't worry, Isaac. In a couple days we will be far enough downriver, and we won't have to worry about being attacked." Chuckling, Oli continued. "And as far as you praying, that I appreciate."

"Oli, what will happen once I am in the mountains? I never thought about the fear before. That's mostly Indian country. Will I be looking around every tree, expecting danger to jump out?"

Oli wished that he had the verbal skills of Frenchy. He could not think of anything to say to Isaac to give him comfort about his future. "Hey, let's go and get some more of those biscuits and jam, Isaac."

Jumping up, Isaac offered a weak smile. "Okay, Oli, sounds like a good idea."

Oli felt that Isaac was glad to break off from the line of conversation. What he had shared was very personal, and for the most part men didn't talk like that.

The men woke to a heavy frost. The world was sparkling in the early morning sun. Oli shook the moisture off his blankets. He noticed that one of his shoes was breaking loose at the sole. Tonight he would get the awl out and fix that. Stowing the blankets on the boat, he then checked the rifles. They were all charged and ready to go. Oli grabbed his mess kit and headed for the cook fire.

Jose and Frenchy were still debating who spit the furthest. Oli saw the stack of pancakes. It wasn't pancake day. He looked over and saw Boss Henry and the boat bosses in a huddle, drawing in the dust with a stick.

Oli had a flashback to his days in the army. Every time they were facing a battle, extra rations were passed out and all the officers were in a huddle. *Just my imagination,* Oli thought. With that, he moved in to get his share of the pancakes.

The rapids proved to be worse than expected with the high water. The boat bosses had everything they could do to keep the boats from running into the rocks. Many were not visible, just under the water, and could hang a boat up. It was impossible to use the push poles for anything but shoving the boat away from obstructions. Boat number four caught briefly on some underwater boulders. Rocking as hard as they could and prying with the push poles, the boat finally broke free.

They continued down the rapids, a quarter-mile behind the other boats. "Get out the oars!" Boss Tuck shouted. "When we get out of these rapids, we will need to row like the devil himself is after us."

Bouncing back and forth, the men stowed the push poles and the oars were readied. When they hit the smooth water, the bow dipped under and they took water. The rifles forward would be useless.

Quickly, the oars were put into the oarlock and the four men put their backs into the work of getting the boat through the narrows and back to the other boats.

As if on cue, the canoes appeared. The Indians' yells were shrill, and the powerful paddlers shot the canoes forward. The fact that they were ready with the oars gave them time to put distance between the Indians and the boat. The gap would close quickly.

Boss Tuck stood with one hand on the tiller and the other with a loaded rifle. He was swearing loudly at the pursuing natives. Releasing the rudder momentarily, he raised the rifle and fired. The ball hit the lead canoe and caused them to hesitate a moment. They then dug in with renewed effort.

The four men continued to strain on their oars. There was a narrow chute in the river that would propel them forward. Boss Tuck was steering toward it. Some of the natives started shooting arrows at them. They fell short for the moment.

"Once we get into the chute, I want you to get the guns and start shooting," Boss Tuck shouted over the cries of the Indians. "The water will carry us downstream and we won't have to worry about steering. Oli, I will need you to load weapons. What we need is rapid reloading."

As though with a trained military unit, the oars were withdrawn as the boat entered the chute. Nobody hesitated as the rifles came up, and as one they fired. Oli was busy reloading the rifles that had gotten wet in the bow. He handed the loaded weapons aft and continued loading as fast as he could.

Arrows were now hitting the boat. The current turned it sideways. This gave the crew a broader field of fire.

"Give 'em a damn broadside, boys!" Boss Tuck shouted.

Oli glanced downstream. The other boats had slowed to allow them to catch up. Oli also saw a group of rocks. If they remained on this course the aft part of the boat would hit them.

"Damn," Oli muttered, "First things first, we have to keep up the firing."

Oli reached out with a loaded rifle and was greeted by a shower of blood. Isaac had been hit in the throat by an arrow and was dead moments after his body hit the bottom of the boat.

Fighting off the desire to scream, Oli kept the loaded weapon and drew down on one of the oncoming natives. Squeezing the trigger, the ball struck the Indian low on the right side. He slumped over and fell into the water.

Half in panic, Oli reloaded the rifle. When he looked up, he could not believe what he saw. The canoes had stopped and were turning towards the fallen Indian floundering in the water.

Things seemed to go into slow motion. Knowing the danger downstream, Oli shouted, "Rocks!" Too late to prevent impact, everyone grabbed a hold.

There was a sickening crash as the stern hit the rocks. The boat spun around, throwing everyone off their feet and breaking loose some of the cargo. Boss Tuck was trying to leap for the rudder when they hit, and he was launched into the water.

Amidst the confusion, Oli managed to get to the stern. He grabbed the rudder shaft. Although it was broken, Oli was able to steer the boat out of the way of additional rocks.

Boat number one came towards them. Frenchy tossed a line and the two boats were lashed together. Boss Tuck had made it to shore and waved that he was okay. Oli looked upstream and could see the Indians retreating.

Tom cried, "Isacc! Isaac! Someone help him." Tom was holding Isaac in his arms. He was trying to remove the arrow. Frenchy moved to Tom to help comfort him.

Boss Henry looked at Oli. "Where are you hit, man?"

Oli was confused for a moment. Boss Henry repeated, "Where are you hit?"

"I'm okay, the blood is Isaac's." Hearing his own words, Oli began to shake.

He had just seen a friend die and was showered in his blood, but hadn't even had a chance to realize it till now. Seeing that Oli was not hurt, Boss Henry began shouting orders to get a boat over to the shore and pick up Boss Tuck.

The boats continued another five miles before Boss Henry felt safe enough to pull in. He found a small cove that was secluded from the river.

"That was a hell of a shot, Oli." Still somewhat dazed, Oli looked up at Boss Tuck. "You hit someone pretty important. You hit him, but did not kill him. He must have been their strong medicine. They had to go back and save him."

"Thank you, boss," Oli responded.

"Damn bad luck about Isaac. I wonder what Tom will do now?" Boss Tuck said.

Oli looked around. "Where is Tom?" He asked.

"He is with Isaac. They cleaned the boy up and he is laid out on a blanket near the edge of the woods," Boss Tuck said, pointing.

"I want to go see Tom," Oli said, standing up.

"You best go and wash the blood off first," Boss Tuck suggested. Nodding, Oli walked to the water's edge.

They laid Isaac to rest near the shores of the small cove. Boss Henry said words over the grave. Tom stood looking on in stony silence. Then it was time to shove off. Oli looked back as the boats were pushed out into the river. A sad and lonely feeling swept over him.

"You know, Frenchy, the next boat that pulls into this cove won't have any idea who is buried under the stones. The next flood season will take the wooden cross away and little will remain of the stones."

"I agree, Oli. The spot will disappear, but as long as we are alive we will remember Isaac," Frenchy said.

Then, spitting over the side and rolling his chaw into the other cheek, Frenchy picked up a push pole. Oli was on watch. Being a man short in the boat, they would be on a three man rotation with two turns on and one off.

Tom stared at the entrance of the cove until it disappeared around the bend. His face was still without expression. No doubt he was still in shock over his brother's death.

Oli reached into his pack and took out his ledger. Trimming up the tip of his pencil, Oli made an entry about Isaac. Just maybe, after everyone on the boat was dead and gone, the ledger would be read by following generations and Isaac would be remembered.

The landing that Boss Henry had promised was everything the men had hoped for, and more. The rye was better than average, the ladies were pretty, and the piano player, Jinx, was a pleasure to listen to.

The next morning Oli sat near the boats, cradling his head in his hands. Jose came over with a cup of coffee and handed it to him.

Oli accepted it gratefully and said, "I believe I just might have had too much fun last night."

Sending a stream of brown tobacco juice towards a foraging field mouse, Jose nodded. "You surely did, Oli. You sung yourself hoarse with that Boston piano player, and the red-headed gal like to dance your legs off. I wouldn't normally coddle a guy that has had too much fun the night before, but you promised to repair boat number four during this stop. That means you got to do it today, and I just wanted to make sure you were up for it."

"Well, I want to thank you, Jose. Don't you worry. I'll have her fixed and good as new for tomorrow."

Boss Tuck had brought some tools over from boat number one. Oli had looked the job over. The rudder would be easy to fix. The stern had taken a good rap against the rocks and would require a bit more. One of the planks had split and needed replacing. While at the cove they had covered the crack with tar.

They had another couple weeks and more than a few rapids to traverse. Without a proper repair the boat would not survive another hit. By noon, Oli was stripped to the waist, and hard at work fitting the new plank. He applied tar to the seam and used wooden pegs to secure the plank.

Tom called Oli to the midday meal, which consisted of freshly baked bread spread generously with butter, pan-fried catfish, and cool buttermilk. It turned out that the ladies they'd spent the night dancing with had four cows. That explained their strong grip when dancing, Oli thought.

Evening found the boats all packed and ready to push off at first light. "Are you going to head up to the saloon for one last rye, Oli?" Tom asked.

"Not tonight, Tom. I enjoyed the saloon last night, but two nights in a row would leave me useless tomorrow. You go ahead and enjoy, Tom. Sing one with Jinx for me and give that redhead a turn on the floor." Oli smiled as he watched Tom head for the saloon.

Tom had a lot to get over, with the loss of his brother. Anything to keep him busy was good. Nothing was to be gained by sitting and brooding about something you could not change.

CHAPTER FIVE

The remainder of the trip on the boats was routine. The water level continued to drop, exposing rocks and sandbars that could have caused problems. On Oli's suggestion, Boss Henry pulled in for a couple days when they reached the Mississippi River.

The four boats were rigged with sails. Taking advantage of a southerly breeze, the trip from the Ohio River to St. Louis was a whole lot easier than rowing or poling against the current.

It was early afternoon when they arrived in St. Louis. It had all the excitement of a western town. The landing area was piled high with goods coming in and going out. Everywhere one looked there were men haggling, trying to get the best prices for what they brought.

Tom stood on the dock with his pack, and Isaac's. Frenchy tossed Oli his packs.

"You take care, Oli. Watch out for those redheaded ladies." Winking, Frenchy turned away and busied himself loosening the cargo tarps.

Picking up his packs and blushing a bit, Oli followed Tom up the dock. Frenchy had given Oli some good-natured advice. Boss Henry had paid each pole man $30 for the trip. Much of what Oli had earned was left at the landing with the redheaded lady.

"Maybe she needed another milk cow," Oli mumbled.

"What did you say?" Tom asked.

Oli shrugged his shoulders. "Nothing, Tom, just giving myself a scolding."

All the extra men were paid and released upon arrival in St. Louis. The rest would help with the unloading and reloading of cargo. Henry Wilson was among the hagglers. He was looking over a large pile of beaver pelts with a skeptical look on his face. After purchasing cargo, he would look for the men needed for the return trip and be off downriver.

Tom stopped and turned to Oli. "I'm still going to the mountains. My brother and I dreamed of becoming trappers too long for me to give it up. I hear they have a rendezvous each year to sell furs and resupply. I plan on being at the one next spring. I would be honored if you would join me."

Shuffling his feet, Oli felt a bit awkward. He could not go with Tom because of his own quest, and he could not tell this to Tom.

"I thank you for the offer, Tom, but I need to complete what brought me here. Who knows what is going to happen? If my trip comes to nothing, maybe I'll be waiting for you at the rendezvous."

"Well, Oli, you will need a gun wherever you're going. I want you to have Isaac's. You were a good friend to me and him. I must admit, I don't know how I would have gotten by without your help."

Oli raised his hand. "No, Tom, you trade it or sell it to buy the Hawken."

Tom thrust the rifle into Oli's hands and, with tears in his eyes, he turned and walked away. Over his shoulder he heard Tom say, "Goodbye, my friend, and safe trip." And Tom was gone, lost in the crowd.

Oli stood there holding the Kentucky long rifle. He knew better than to follow Tom. It would only embarrass him to show so much emotion. To no one in particular, Oli softly said, "And may you be safe and happy on your journey."

It was the end of April. The grass was green and the breezes warm as Oli made his way through the crowded streets of St. Louis. He noticed a large oak tree on the bank of a creek. It was just outside of town and he was glad to find a quiet place.

It was time to take stock. Looking over the ledger, Oli smiled. He wouldn't need too much before joining a wagon train. Licking the end of the pencil, he added one rifle. He would need to get some powder and shot.

Looking around to make sure that there were no prying eyes, Oli opened his money belt. He counted $57.42.

Grinning, he thought out loud. "It could have been $87.42 if I had only worked on fixing the boat both days."

Oli decided to spend the first night right there under the oak tree. Setting up the tent, he looked for something to put under the ground tarp. He shoved leaves under the tarp, patted his hand on it and smiled.

Striking the flint with the back of his knife, it sent a shower of sparks into the tinder he had gathered. Soon he had a nice blaze going. While the days were warm in late April, the nights were cool. He enjoyed the warmth of the fire as he put the coffee pot to boil.

He had had to walk back into town and get water from the town pump. When he'd looked closely at the creek, he hadn't been sure if it was water or something else. He'd guessed someone had watered stock upstream.

Oli sat against the tree, sipping his coffee and watching the sun set on the plain. The sky was multiple shades of red, with the sun a large ball on the horizon. After the sun set, Oli looked at the lights of St. Louis. Getting up to bank his fire, Oli looked to the west. Dotting the area were flickering lights of campfires. Grabbing a limb, Oli swung up and climbed the tree. He estimated that the furthest fires were up to two miles away.

Suddenly he was concerned. How on earth would he find the train he needed to go west? Sliding down, Oli crawled into his blankets. Tomorrow he would go into town and find someone who could help him.

It was getting light when Oli rolled out of his blankets. A soft drizzle was coming down. He looked at his nicely banked fire, which was now soggy ash. Checking his coffee pot, he had about half a cup of cold brew. Breakfast was taking small drinks of the cold coffee and chewing a piece of hard bread.

Sitting under the tent, Oli removed the deerskin coat from a pack and slipped it on. Wrapped in his coat and sitting on his blankets, Oli evaluated the situation. First, he would find a boarding house and some hot coffee, then he would make inquiries about a wagon train.

Carefully tearing a page out of the ledger, Oli drew the treasure map from memory, leaving the location of the gold off. He decided that he would show it around, saying that he was going to meet a trapper friend. If someone recognized the area he could then ask about wagon trains.

With his packs on his back, the rifle cradled in his arm and his coat buttoned all the way up, Oli walked back into St. Louis. He found a hotel with a common sleeping room. It had beds for twelve men and cost 25 cents per night, including breakfast. Oli tossed his packs onto a top bunk. Taking the ledger out of a pack, he put it into his coat pocket.

Stopping at the desk, Oli asked the clerk, "Too late for coffee?"

Not bothering to look up, the clerk said, "Yup, too late."

Oli fought the desire to rap the clerk on the head with the barrel of the long rifle. He stepped out the door. The light drizzle was now a steady rain. The street was quickly turning to a sea of mud. With the rain running down the back of his neck, he decided that his first stop was the mercantile.

Pushing open the door, his senses were overwhelmed with smells of coffee, leather goods, new rope, oils, and so many other things. He stood just inside the door with his eyes closed for a moment.

"Can I help you with something?" Looking over, Oli saw the elderly, slightly bald, bespectacled owner.

Moving up to the counter, Oli paused to look around the store. "I need to buy a hat that will keep the rain out from my neck."

"I certainly can help you with that," the storekeeper said, moving quickly to the shelf in the back. "How much are you looking to spend?"

"Well," Oli said, "I don't have a lot to spend. I am going out on a wagon train."

"Hmmm, I think I know just what you want. This should fit you."

Picking a round-topped hat with a flat brim, the storekeeper handed it to Oli. Oli placed it on his

59

head and looked at his reflection in the window. Adjusting it a bit to improve the fit, Oli nodded.

"How much is it?"

"That one would be one dollar," the shopkeeper replied, hurrying back to his counter.

Oli removed two half dollar coins from the money belt.

"You need any dry powder for that old flint lock?" the storekeeper asked with a half-smile.

"Now that you mentioned it, I will need a powder horn and some bullets," Oli said, wiping some of the rain off the long rifle with his sleeve.

"You'll need some gun oil and some patches also, unless you got them" the storekeeper said confidently. It was early and a slow day, so he figured that he could sell this fellow plenty.

"Tell you what, I will put a list together and bring it to you once I hook up with a wagon train," Oli said, turning to leave the store.

"We'll be here. I'll make sure you get the best prices in St. Louis," the disappointed storekeeper called after him.

Kicking the mud off his boots, Oli stopped in front of the sheriff's office. Walking in, Oli shook the water off his new hat. He frowned briefly as he looked at the now soggy hat. Oli walked up to the stocky sheriff sitting at a somewhat scuffed desk littered with posters.

The sheriff stared at Oli, waiting for him to speak. "Would you be Sheriff Tate? A fellow up the street said I could find you here."

"That I am," grunted the sheriff.

"Could you recommend a wagon train?"

Oli handed the drawn map to the sheriff. "I am supposed to meet up with a trapper named Tom Franklin in this area," Oli said, pointing to where the mountains and a river met.

The sheriff studied the map for a moment. Leaning back in his chair, the sheriff looked up. "I would recommend you continue to Independence. You'll find more wagon trains heading out from there."

"My hope is that I could find one heading out from here," Oli replied.

The sheriff continued to study the map while Oli waited. "My guess it would be the Platte River. Course, it could be the Arkansas River, but my understanding is that the Platte goes more east and west."

Still scrutinizing the map, the sheriff reflected. "Had a guy come through here heading back east some years back. He talked of Spanish gold somewhere in that area. You might be better off to forget your trapper friend and go look for the gold."

Laughing, the sheriff slapped his knee. Startled by the comment, Oli laughed with the sheriff. Oli noticed Sheriff Tate had a pot of coffee on the potbelly stove.

Trying to change the subject, Oli asked, "You wouldn't happen to have any extra coffee, would you?"

"Sure do, help yourself."

Oli poured a cup of the strong brew. After breathing deep of the aroma, he took a sip. "Thank you, sheriff. I started out this morning with a waterlogged camp fire. This is the first hot drink I have had today."

"You wouldn't be the fellow that was camping near the oak just out of town, would you?"

Oli nodded, enjoying the hot coffee.

"Well, I hope you didn't drink out of that creek. Part of the town dumps its sewage upstream from the tree. That would make you a right stout cup of coffee." The sheriff was really laughing now.

Hacking and coughing while he laughed, the sheriff finally cleared his throat and looked at Oli. "After you finish your coffee, you might want to go a bit south of town and look up a group headed up by Jack Alberts. My understanding is he is pulling out next week and should be passing pretty close to where you want to go."

Debating on whether he should have another cup of coffee or not, Oli finally set the cup down and turned towards the door. "Thanks, sheriff. And thanks for the coffee, it was good and hot."

Oli had no trouble finding Jack Alberts' camp. Several of the town folks knew of him and continued to direct Oli in the right direction. The rain continued to fall, and Oli was pleased that the once new hat was doing its job.

He found their camp about a mile south of town. Jack was sitting under a fly tarp, just about to have his noon meal. Dipping his bread into a plate full of beans, Jack took a big bite and turned to Oli while he chewed.

Wiping his mouth with the back of his hand, he nodded to the cook fire. "Help yourself to some of the best beans south of St. Louis. They told me you were looking for a group going west."

Gratefully, Oli scooped a generous portion of beans onto a plate. Picking up a piece of bread, he walked back under the tarp.

"That I am, sir. I am headed to the point where the Platte intersects the mountains." Both men sat quietly, enjoying their meal for a bit.

"Coffee?" Jack offered.

"Yes, thank you."

Oli filled a cup with coffee and couldn't help but pick up another slice of bread. Sitting back down and dunking the bread into the coffee, Oli swallowed it in big bites.

Staring at his hungry guest, Jack grinned. "I hope the heck I won't have to feed you on the trip."

Drinking the last of his coffee Oli apologized. "I am sorry. With the rain, breakfast was less than satisfying. You do serve a fine meal."

Leaning back, Jack asked Oli, "What type of outfit will you be driving?"

Confused for a moment, Oli frowned. "I won't be driving a wagon. I have packs with all the stuff I would need."

Smiling, Jack said, "Maybe we should start over. I have several requirements on my wagon trains. Granted, not everyone who goes on the train has a team and wagon. Everyone must have a good horse, provisions for six weeks, a rifle and the knowledge of how to shoot, powder and balls for 100 shots, and the fee payable in advance. You must also have enough money to replenish along the way."

"What is the fee?" Oli asked.

"Les see." Jack thought for a minute. "You'd just be going to the mountains, so . . . how does twenty dollars sound?"

Like a lot of money, Oli thought. To Jack he said, "Sounds fair. I got some buying to do. I will be back tomorrow to see you. Thanks again for the food."

Oli left the wagon master and hurried back to town. Looking up, he saw the sky was clearing. The mud on the street was now ankle-deep. Oli could feel it oozing through the sole of his boot.

"Guess I didn't sew those stitches tight enough when I was on the boat," he muttered, shaking his left foot.

Leaning against the porch post in front of the mercantile, Oli scraped the mud from his boots. Oli figured that he could spend $15 on goods. He would need a new pair of boots, powder, balls, patches, gun oil, another pair of socks, and some grub.

The storekeeper smiled as Oli walked in. "You got that list made?"

"It will be a short list," Oli replied, "I have limited funds, and certain things I have to get to go with Jack Alberts' group."

"He's a good man to travel with. Yes sir, a good man, but he is strict about what each participant brings along," the storekeeper said with a widening smile.

For the next hour, Oli and the storekeeper went over the items that would be needed. Several were selected and later rejected because of cost. It was late afternoon when Oli left the store. He had spent $14.30. He must have softened the heart of the storekeeper, because as he was leaving the storekeeper tossed him a small bag of birdshot.

"Here, take this. You just might need it to eat."

Oli thanked him and stepped out the door. The sun was peeking out of the clouds with the promise of better weather. Shifting the burlap bags on his back, Oli headed for the hotel. Walking into the room, Oli noticed that his packs had been moved on his bunk.

A big bruiser was dozing two bunks down. His feet with holey socks hung off the end due to his height. A quick check of the packs showed that nothing was missing, but it was evident that they had been gone through. Oli placed the bags next to his packs. One bag contained beans, hard bread, and a small amount of jerky. The other contained things necessary for his long rifle, and a new pair of boots.

Taking his knife out Oli carved an "O" into the heel of each boot. It was a habit he picked up on the ocean crossing. Many sailors' boots looked alike and it prevented them from getting mixed up.

Taking the powder horn and putting some balls, flint, and patches in a small sack, he tied it around the powder horn strap. Oli slung it around his neck and arm. He liked the feel of it at his side. The long rifle he was carrying was a weapon. Now it was time to see about a horse. With this thought in mind, Oli headed for the livery stable.

Oli entered the big doors and was confronted with a string of first-class cussing and shouting from the back of the barn. Still grumbling, a short, stooped man limped out of the shadows.

"Damn donkey, it stepped squarely on my foot. Then it pinned me against the stall. Was all I could do to push him away."

The livery hostler looked over at Oli. Giving Oli a broad, toothless smile, he asked, "What do you need, young man?"

"I need to purchase a horse," Oli replied.

Standing on one foot, the hostler removed the other boot and started rubbing his injured foot, "Gonna lose a damn toenail from this one. You know, horse flesh is hard to come by with all the demand up in Independence."

"I understand that, but I need to get a horse so I can join Jack Alberts' group," Oli said, looking down the row of stalls, "I have $15 and was told a man could buy a decent pack animal for that."

"Maybe back east or in the South, but not in St. Louis. If I were you I would go back to whoever told you that and buy you a horse from him," replied the hostler.

Slapping his knee, the hostler suddenly turned. "Follow me, laddie, I just might have an animal for you. It's out back in the corral."

Walking out the side door and leaning on the rails, he continued. "I just got this one in from a fellow heading to New Orleans. She's got a few years on her and most of her teeth. The shoes are tight and I can let you have her for $15. I will even give you a bridle."

"How old is a few years?" Oli inquired.

"Now you can't judge a horse by its age. This one is nigh on to 30 years, give or take a bit. But the condition is damn good for $15. One other thing young man, this may be the only horse you will find in St. Louis for the price you are willing to pay. She's a good horse."

With that, the hostler turned back towards the barn. Oli followed, knowing that he had been bested by the old gent. Oli was able to negotiate one more night's boarding for the good horse at the livery. He was also able to get it moved into a stall and fed a bait of oats.

Oli got back to the hotel. He noticed the big bruiser was gone. The next thing he noticed was that his new boots were gone.

Running from the room to the front desk, Oli shouted at the clerk, "Where is the louse that was sleeping in the room?"

"He decided not to stay. I told him no refunds. He did not complain," replied the clerk as he continued to stare at his newspaper.

Grabbing the clerk by his shirt, Oli pulled him half across the desk. "I need the shoes he took in order to go west. I cannot afford another pair. So far I have not found St. Louis a hospitable town!"

Shoving the clerk back against the wall, Oli immediately felt remorse. He knew that this man was not guilty of anything more than indifference. Taking a deep breath, Oli held up both of his hands to assure the clerk that there was no more anger being vented in his direction.

"I apologize for grabbing you. As I said, I need to get the boots back. Can you tell me where the man that left may have gone?"

Adjusting his shirt and slicking back his disheveled hair, the clerk regained his lofty attitude. "I can do better than that. I know where he went. But I should warn you, the louse as you called him is a mean one."

"He is known to have crushed a man's spine over a disagreement of how he wore his hat. I dare not guess how many killings he has to his name. You are welcome to confront him about the boots, but I can well guess you will just be another on his list of killings. You will find him at the Lucky Lady saloon. He will no doubt be there until very late."

Turning away, the clerk rustled the newspaper a bit and continued to read.

Oli crossed the street to the Lucky Lady muttering, "Damn mud."

His boots created a sucking sound with each step. Oli believed forewarned is being prepared. Rather than bursting into the saloon, Oli stopped at the door and looked the room over.

He could see the man standing at the bar, nursing a shot of whiskey. On his feet were a nice new pair of boots, now somewhat muddied. He wore a cap and ball revolver on his right hip and a knife on his left. He had a permanent scowl on his whiskered face.

Oli went back to the hotel and checked his packs and bags. All were in order. His long rifle lay where he left it. He debated the course of action. He could challenge the man in the saloon and probably die doing so. It would solve his need for the new boots.

Not a good solution. Or, he could shoot the man for being a thief. He was sure that the local sheriff would not arrest him for shooting a thief. Of course, he might only wound him and in turn the man would shoot him with the ball and cap revolver. Once again being dead, his need for the boots would be gone.

Oli frowned and muttered. "Also not a good solution."

Leaving his rifle and the packs on his bunk, Oli walked back to the clerk's desk. At least he now looked up when Oli approached.

"If the man does not plan to come back here to sleep, where do you think he will go?"

"To the livery stable, more than likely." The clerk turned and adjusted the lamp behind the desk.

Oli looked at the darkening streets and made up his mind. "I will be checking out also," he said to the clerk.

Without looking his way the clerk said, "No refunds."

Oli picked up his packs and bags from his bunk. Hefting them on his back, he was sure that they weighed 200 pounds. Cradling the long rifle in his arms, he left the hotel and went to the livery stable. The hostler was nowhere to be seen.

He went to the stall of his good horse and settled down to wait. Oli was dozing off and on when he heard someone stumble in. Cursing and belching, the man climbed into the hay loft. Oli heard the clunk of the boots being taken off. In a matter of minutes he could hear loud snoring.

Without delay Oli moved out of the stall, leaving his packs next to the good horse. Slowly, he crept up the ladder. The creak of the rungs almost stopped his heart. Softly, he crawled across the loft floor.

There they were. His boots were lying next to the man with holey sock-covered feet. Quietly, Oli felt for the "O's" on the heels. They were there. He lifted the boots and moved back to the ladder. His heart pounding in his chest, Oli descended the ladder.

Struggling to get his packs on his back and laying the bags of goods across the good horse's back, Oli moved out of the barn. He tucked a good amount of hay under his arm as he left. No doubt he looked a sight loaded down with packs, hay, and his rifle while he led a horse carrying just two bags.

Oli went to the outside of town, back to the oak tree. Setting everything down, he staked the good horse a bit away from the stream. Leaving the hay within its reach, he settled down under the tree, wrapped in his deerskin coat for a restless night of sleep.

He spent the night dreaming of being confronted by the big bruiser over and over again. Never was Oli so happy to see morning come. Chewing on hard bread and a bit of jerky, he designed a rack to hold the packs on the good horse's back. Setting about with his knife, some oak branches, and some leather strings from his pack, Oli fashioned a first-class sawbuck rig to carry the packs on the good horse.

Then taking a bit of time, Oli took out the ledger. It was time to take an accounting of his assets:

2 wool shirts, 2 wool pants, 3 pair woolen socks, 2 long underwear,2 pair boots, 1 darning needle,1 leather awl, 1 whetstone, 1

knife, 1 razor, 1 roll of leather, 1 wool blanket, 1 deerskin coat, light duty rope, 1 fine hat, 1 belt, 1 ground canvas, 1 tent, 2 flints, 1 coffee pot, 1 cook pot, 1 canteen, 6 fish hooks, 1 Kentucky long rifle, 1 powder horn, food for 3 weeks (beans, coffee, jerky, flour), 1 mess kit (cup, plate, bowl, spoon), powder, ball, oil, patches, and bird shot, 1 good horse with bridle

Looking over the list, Oli was not as pleased as in the past. He knew his money belt now held the $20 for the wagon train fee and that left only $6.87. It was a small amount to begin such a long trip.

The sun said that it was a bit after mid-morning when Oli, wearing his new boots, led the good horse toward Jack Alberts' group. He was just out of town when he heard shouting and cussing coming from the direction of the livery stable. He jumped a bit when he heard the shot from the man's revolver. Picking up the pace, he continued south to the camp.

Jack Alberts looked Oli and his outfit over. "Mr. August, do you know what is in store for this wagon train over the next several months?"

"Yes, I do . . ."

Jack interrupted him. "I do not think you do. That horse you have there is on its last legs. The tendon is swollen in the front left leg. If it has half its teeth you would be lucky. It will be living on buffalo grass which is tough enough to eat with a full set of teeth. My guess is you couldn't get more than fifty cents for the hide, and that is all it is worth. You don't have half the food required and you will be forced to walk all the way to the mountains. That horse will be lucky to be able to carry your gear, much less you and your gear."

If Oli had ever looked upon a disgusted face, he was now looking at one. His fear was that this was the end of the road, until he could save up enough money to buy a proper outfit.

"Mr. Alberts, I appreciate your assessment of my outfit, but I must defend my good horse. Yes, she is old, but her shoes are tight and she has most of her teeth. She is in good weight to start the trip. I will get some oats to make sure her strength remains. I, in turn, have walked all of my life and am sure I could keep the pace with your train. I have money left to get more food. My hope is you would reconsider and allow me to join you."

Oli also figured it would be unhealthy for him to show up back in town with his new boots.

Jack Alberts stood there rubbing his chin. "Can you shoot the rifle?"

Oli knew that he meant shoot and hit something. Now Oli wished that he had shot the gun a bit to know which way it might drift.

Knowing that nothing was to be gained by the truth, Oli nodded. "I managed to come through quite a scrap on the Ohio when Indians attacked our boats."

Jack picked up a chunk of wood and, walking about 20 paces from the camp, set it on an ant hill. Coming back, Jack appraised the target.

"Load your rifle and hit that piece of wood. If you do and if you come up with the food, you will be welcome to join the train."

Oli measured the powder in the barrel. Wrapping a greased patch around the ball, he then rammed it down the barrel. He took his time and was quite deliberate. Not so much for any reason other than to give his hands a bit of time to stop shaking. He realized that he had meant to clean and oil the rifle, but with all that had gone on he had not had the chance. Priming the pan with a bit of powder, Oli looked over at the chunk of wood.

Saying a short prayer, Oli raised the rifle and squeezed off the shot. He felt the sharp impact of the recoil as he watched the chunk of wood skip away.

"Well done, Oli, now go and get your food. We leave in three days."

Relief flooded over Oli. He turned to place the rifle with his packs.

"I saw the prayer," Jack said, smiling. "You can put your '*good*' horse with the rest of the stock. Set your tent up anywhere you want. You are welcome to share my cook fire."

Hesitating a moment, he then dug into his gear. Pulling out a well-worn canvas bag, he tossed it to Oli. "Here's a possible bag to stow your stuff. You'll be dead before you can undo the bag you got."

Oli picked up some oats from the livery. He mentioned the swollen tendon. The hostler seemed anxious to have him gone and gave him a very good price on the oats. With the oats over his shoulder, Oli headed for the camp.

He passed a barefooted farmer pushing a cart filled with potatoes. "Going to market with the potatoes?" Oli asked.

"I am indeed," responded the farmer.

"I was wondering if you and I could do a bit of trading?" Oli asked, hefting a potato in his hand.

By mid-afternoon of the last day, Oli had a bag of 67 potatoes and one less pair of boots. Oli had to re-sole the boots prior to completing the deal. That night at the fire, as Oli slowly roasted a potato, Jack reminded him that they would be pulling out at first light in the morning.

"Hello, the camp." A voice came out of the dark.

A lone horseman rode up. Oli's heart all but stopped. It was *the man!*

Jack walked over and extended his hand to the rider. "I am glad you decided to join us. A good scout can make the trip much easier."

Shaking his hand firmly, the bruiser swung down. Oli sat next to the fire, rubbing ash over his new boots. Oli noted the man also had new boots. They were riding boots, as opposed to the low-heeled work boots that Oli had.

Jack brought the man over to the fire. "This here is Oli August. He is one of my marksmen. Oli, this is Bart Nevell, our scout for this trip."

Flustered with the meeting, and never before having been called a marksman, Oli extended his hand. "How do you do . . . Bart?"

Bart furled his heavy eyebrows as he looked at Oli. "I am looking forward to watching your skill with the long gun on this trip."

Oli's hand ached from the firm shake. Sitting back down, he busied himself with the potato as Bart and Jack took cups of coffee and moved off to the side to discuss the trip.

Oli figured that if Bart did recognize him, he would no doubt leave his lifeless body lying somewhere along the route. If he did not recognize him, Oli decided that he would give this man no reason to want to kill him.

CHAPTER SIX

It was the first week of May when they pulled out. Daylight found everyone awake and ready to go. Jack rode past the wagons, telling each one what position they would have in the train. The position of each wagon would change from day to day, providing some relief from the dust as it moved to the front.

Bart Nevell had gotten up early and had already moved out to check the trail. They would be following the Missouri River to Independence. There, Jack hoped to pick up some additional wagons. Then the wagon train would continue until they got to the Platte River. It would then follow the river until they reached the mountains.

Oli would leave the train at the mountains, and the rest would continue through the South Pass and on to Oregon. Only a few years earlier, the first wagon train of 20 wagons, led by Captain Benjamin Bonneville, had made it through the pass.

Oli had sorted his packs, deciding what would go on the good horse and what would go on the pack on his back. Once done, the pack on the good horse was approximately 200 pounds. His pack was just over 100 pounds. He had made a scabbard for the long rifle on the good horse's pack rigging. It was tipped forward so he could get to it in short order.

With a good walking stick in one hand and the lead rope in the other, Oli took his place in the train. The eight wagons and Oli's good horse slowly strung out as they started west.

The morning was a lot of starts and stops, as everyone was getting used to staying in line. Oli found himself standing and waiting as much as walking. After a quick noon meal, the train pulled out again. It appeared that the morning lessons were learned and the train moved more smoothly.

Evening found them 12 miles from St. Louis. Jack circled the wagons. There was not a great fear of hostiles, but rather the gathering of the wagons made controlling the stock much easier.

Early summer was blooming everywhere. Oli enjoyed seeing the new leaves on the trees and wild flowers dotting the hillsides. They were traveling along the Missouri River Valley. Grass was plentiful for the stock. Oli had seen some game, but after the confusion of the first day, he decided to start hunting once a routine was established.

Oli was just finishing setting up his tent when Mrs. Weber, from the wagon in front of him, came over. "Mr. Weber and I would like to invite you to join us for supper tonight."

Looking up at the portly lady, Oli thanked her for the invite. Mrs. Weber continued to stand there. Oli stopped what he was doing and looked up.

"It is generally proper to offer something for the soup pot when invited."

"Oh, yes, of course," Oli replied.

"Some taters would be good," Mrs. Weber said. "Say, maybe six."

Doing some quick math in his head Oli, knew that he couldn't really afford to spare that much food for one meal. But to be sociable, he opened the potato sack and selected six small potatoes. He handed them to Mrs. Weber.

She took them and snorted, "Hope you didn't pay too much for these sickly little taters. Supper is in an hour."

Oli continued to make things a bit more comfortable, and then he walked to the creek to wash up. Walking to the Webers' fire, he could see Mr. and Mrs. Weber and their three children busily eating.

"Soup's in the pot and coffee is on the edge of the fire," Mrs. Weber called out.

Taking his bowl to the pot, Oli took hold of the ladle. A quick stir of the pot proved that there was little potato left and nothing else in the soup. Looking around, there was not any bread or biscuits. Filling his bowl with broth and a few bits of potato,

Oli then filled his cup with coffee. He could see the bottom of the cup.

Looking over, he noticed Mr. Weber stick the last piece of biscuit in his mouth. Oli sat on a log next to their youngest boy. The children needed their hands and faces washed. Their clothes were in disrepair.

Oli hurriedly drank down the soup. He then drank the weak coffee. With his stomach still growling, he thanked the family and went back to his camp. Sitting in the dark, he chewed on a piece of hard bread.

"I think I will always be busy at supper time from now on," Oli sighed.

The next morning, the wagon train was rolling as the sun came up. Jack Alberts was hoping to make no less than 15 miles a day. He kept the wagons moving at a good pace, hoping to establish a faster speed for the following days.

Oli was following the Miller wagon. Wink Miller was sitting tall on the seat and humming as the wagon rocked on.

Oli charged the long rifle with bird shot and led the good horse a hundred yards to the south of the wagons. He was able to knock down two prairie chickens during the morning. The river basin narrowed during the afternoon, so Oli put the rifle in its scabbard and fell in behind the Millers.

Wink Miller's wife had died during his trip from Virginia to St. Louis. This left Wink alone to raise his

10 year-old son Michael. Oli liked Wink and his son. He decided to share the prairie chickens with Mr. Miller. He walked along side Wink.

Tossing the two prairie chickens up to him, Oli smiled. "Join me for supper tonight?"

Picking up one of the birds, Wink looked it over. "Happy to. You got the birds, we'll clean them and do the cooking."

Wink's brow wrinkled as he looked at Oli's pack. "Hand that up here, Oli. No sense of you carrying the pack. This area is easy pulling and we got room in the wagon."

Oli thanked Wink and handed the pack up. Waving, Oli fell back into line behind Wink. Without the pack, he felt like he was floating along. He noticed that the good horse was favoring the front leg. Oli removed the rifle and powder horn from the pack. He also removed the bedroll, which had his blanket, ground tarp, tent, and deerskin coat. He slung these over his shoulder. Oli couldn't tell for sure, but he thought that the good horse was limping less.

Jack pulled the wagon train into a small clearing just before sunset. With the wagons in a circle, the cook fires began to spring up. After stripping the pack, Oli took the good horse down to the creek and let her have some water. He let her have a good roll. Picketing her on a patch of lush grass, Oli squatted down to check on the front leg. The tendons were still swollen, but there wasn't any inflammation in the area.

In the background, he could hear Mrs. Weber calling his name. Oli sat in the gathering shadows and waited until he saw Mrs. Weber begin cooking. He then wandered over to the Miller fire.

Wink smiled. "I heard your supper partner calling you."

Wink was busy basting the two birds on his spit. He had a Dutch oven on the edge of his fire. It smelled like corn bread to Oli. When Wink bent over to check the corn bread, Oli noticed the handle of a knife under his collar. Oli had seen this before. Most often it was a throwing knife.

"Bring your plate, and come and get it," Wink called over.

His son Michael was busy setting up a makeshift table. The three of them dug into the food with little talk. The prairie chicken was crisp on the outside and the meat was juicy. The corn bread was moist with a hint of sweet to it. Wink had molasses to pour over the corn bread.

With the meal eaten and the dishes done, the two men sat drinking nice, strong coffee. It had a taste Oli didn't recognize.

"It's mixed with chicory," Wink offered. "Chicory is more available out west, and cheaper than coffee. It helps stretch the coffee. Once the coffee is gone the chicory is a good substitute."

Oli took another drink. "I'll be darned if that isn't a good tasting brew."

The men continued to sip their coffee while they watched young Michael climb into the wagon to go to sleep.

"Are you good with the knife?" Oli asked.

"Good enough. They call me Wink because I can throw the knife as quick as a wink and usually hit what I am throwing at." Wink took the knife out and showed it to Oli.

Oli pulled his knife and compared it to Wink's. "Not a lot different, Wink," Oli said.

"If you want, I can do a little work with yours and make it a first-rate throwing knife," Wink commented, hefting Oli's knife.

Wink suddenly flipped his wrist, and Oli's knife flashed out towards a log 15 feet away and split a beetle that was crawling along.

"Yes, you have a well-balanced knife there." Smiling, he walked over to the log and removed the knife.

Wink and Oli continued to talk for another hour before turning in. Oli stopped and checked on the good horse before heading for his tent, then snuggled down in his blanket. Two days down and oh-so-many more to go.

The daily routine seemed endless. Early morning starts, quick noon meal stops, late afternoon circling of the wagons for the night. This left little time for taking care of the stock and having supper. Oli had continued success avoiding Mrs. Weber. Most often he ate alone.

Wink insisted Oli put the oats and potatoes in the wagon. That left a pack on the good horse weighing less than 100 pounds. The limp on the front leg disappeared.

Some days Oli would tie his horse to Wink's wagon. This allowed him to range farther out to hunt. He generally bagged some small game to share with the various wagons.

One day he noticed a deer lying under an evergreen. The gun was already loaded with birdshot. Oli moved slowly, stalking the deer, which was enjoying the sunshine filtering through the branches. Coming from the upwind side, Oli got about 30 feet away. He took careful aim and fired at the deer's head. Stunned, the deer floundered and Oli jumped forward. Pulling his knife, he slit the deer's throat before it got its wits about it.

Walking back to the wagon train with the deer across his shoulders, Oli tossed it into the back of Wink's wagon. That night, he cut the deer up and shared it with the other wagons. Mrs. Weber thanked him, but it did not come with an offer of supper.

Jack Alberts came over and sat with Oli. Oli was just finishing up roasting some venison steaks over the fire. He offered some meat and coffee to Jack. Jack pulled some biscuits wrapped in a cloth from his shirt and offered one to Oli.

They sat eating and watching the activity around the camp. "Everyone appreciates the meat you bring in. Bart even commented on your good shooting."

Oli smiled. "That is high praise, coming from Bart Nevell."

He had not seen much of Bart, who was gone before daylight scouting the trail, then camped off by himself in the evening. Bart said it allowed him to listen to the night better. Each evening he gave his recommendation to Jack, and was off to his camp.

After modifying Oli's knife, Wink started teaching him to throw. The only modification that was needed was filing the hand protector down so it would slide out of the sheath without catching. Oli modified his sheath to carry the knife down the nape of his neck, like Wink. It made grasping and delivering the knife much faster. Oli spent his evenings on the trail, practicing the art of knife throwing. He enjoyed watching the blade streak toward its target

Independence was busy, and expensive. Camp fires dotted the prairie, with people waiting to join a wagon train. Jack wanted to stay there no more than four days. It was enough time to give everyone a rest, but not enough time for them to find another train to join up with.

The day they arrived, another wagon master met with Jack Alberts. Oli saw him pointing at a wagon. A woman with a bonnet covering her blond hair bent over the cook pot. Two young girls sat, watching her prepare the meal. He saw Mr. Alberts look at his and Wink's camp.

After supper that first night, Oli gave the good horse a thorough rubdown. He noticed that Wink and young Michael were eating at the blond woman's camp.

Oli kept busy the four days, assisting in repairs around the camp. One wagon split an axle on a rock when the driver dozed off and let the team drift from the trail. Oli found a spare axle, and with a little modification he was able to fit it to the wagon.

After each repair, Oli found that he was invited to join the family for supper. He was able to leave Independence without having to buy any goods.

Bart would go into town every night and return late with a load on. Oli stayed clear, just in case the drinking cleared Bart's mind and reminded him where he'd first met him.

Up until Independence, wood had been plentiful. Each wagon had its own fire and often burned it late. Going forward, things would be different. Jack instructed each family to sling a canvas under the wagon and asked that they walk some and toss buffalo chips or any wood they found into the canvas. This fuel would be shared in the common fire. Each wagon would save enough for a small breakfast fire.

Jack was able to pick up seven more wagons. One family dropped out due to illness. That would make 14 wagons, plus Oli.

The blond woman's name was Eve. She had lost her husband during a river crossing. She was slim, with long blond hair, which was kept in a bun. Eve's hazel eyes twinkled when she smiled. Her face and hands showed the stress and hard work of the trip. The two small girls were her daughters.

Often times it was need, rather than love, that would bring couples together. The two wagon masters had introduced Wink and Eve. He had lost his wife, and she needed a husband, to continue the trip west. None of the wagon trains would take a woman with young children on such a difficult trip.

Wink and Eve felt an attraction to each other, which was a benefit. A quick wedding was held and the people from the wagon train held a celebration for the newlyweds.

A few instruments were brought out. A couple of jugs appeared and were shared. Some of the ladies made a pretty darn good cake to be enjoyed by all.

Morning came with a steady drizzle. It didn't put a damper on the mood of anyone. The wedding party the night before left everyone with spirits elevated. Despite the rain, one could hear laughter and joking around the camp.

Wink came over to Oli's tent and joined him for coffee. "I see you got some chicory," Wink said, taking a sip of the coffee. "I could smell it as I brought the cup to my lips."

"Thanks for noticing, Wink. I have been keeping my eyes open for it." Oli offered some hard bread to Wink.

"Oli, I came here to discuss something with you. Eve has a wagon with stuff she doesn't want to leave behind. I need someone to help with the driving. Would you be willing to drive her wagon? The good horse could be tied to the back. You could carry your stuff in the wagon and the horse would be in better condition at the end of trip. Michael could drive the wagon when you are off hunting."

Oli sat there for moment, thinking. "I'd be happy to, Wink. You know, I only plan to go to the mountains. What will you do after that?"

Wink poured a bit more coffee. "Eve will then drive her wagon. Once again, Michael will be able to relieve her. You driving the wagon until then will leave her less tired for the final leg."

Oli looked over Eve's wagon. It was in excellent shape. Oli packed his stuff into the wagon. The good horse seemed happy to be following without a pack. Oli was in the third wagon position the first day out of Independence. He was enjoying the view from higher up. The team handled well. The rain had stopped, prairie flowers were springing up everywhere, and everything smelled fresh.

Three weeks out of Independence, Jack Alberts called everyone together for a meeting. Bart had spotted some unshod pony tracks. They would follow the wagon train for a while and then ride off. Bart did not think that it was the same Indians each time. The Indians might be Pawnee or Lakota.

Jack didn't think the train was in immediate danger of being attacked, but he did want everyone to keep their weapons loaded and handy. The wagon train was now on an open prairie, with buffalo grass as far as the eye could see. The prairie was dotted with trees that grew along rivers and streams. Herds of buffalo were spotted each day.

One day, Oli had young Michael drive the team and he walked ahead of the wagon train. He was about a mile out when he saw a young buffalo bull rolling in a wallow. Getting as close as he could, Oli took careful aim at the shoulder and squeezed off a shot. The animal grunted and slumped over.

By the time the wagon train caught up, Oli was almost done skinning the bull. Several men joined him to cut it up. Everyone would be eating meat tonight. Bart came down over a swell and looked at the bull.

"You got yourself a nice hide, Oli."

"Well, Bart, I got no way of carrying it after the mountains. You are welcome to the hide if you want."

Dismounting, Bart walked up and took hold of the hide. "You know, I think I will." Lifting the folded hide, Bart placed it on the rump of his horse and lashed it to the saddle. He rode back to the wagon where he stored his gear.

The meat was quickly divided up, and the wagon train was once again on its way. A couple days later, Wink called over to Oli.

"See what Bart did with the wagon his stuff is in? He covered the sides with the buffalo hide."

Oli nodded. "I noticed it also. I asked Jack about it, and he said Bart was reinforcing the sides in case of an attack."

Wink looked at the horizon. "I wonder if Bart knows something we don't. I guess we best keep our eyes open."

The trip from Independence to the mountains was estimated to take two months. The wagon train was about halfway and now following the Platte River. The lush, thick prairie grasses had changed to sparser buffalo grass, prairie switch grass, tumbleweed, and wild flowers. Groves of cottonwood and oak grew along the river. The blowing wind was a constant, often driving dust clouds through the wagon train.

The wagon train planned to stop when they passed a trading post. While meat was available from buffalo and whitetail deer, other items would be available at the posts. It was late afternoon when a long, low building came into view. Its walls were log, the roof was thatched prairie grass. There was a corral to one side with some half-wild horses with mustang mix. Jack Alberts decide that it was a good place to spend the night.

The trading post was stocked surprisingly well. They had leather goods, gingham cloth, pails, tools, and odds and ends that made life a bit better. They also had salt and flour, jerky, some canned goods, and a barrel of pickles. To one side, the trading post had a makeshift bar and sold rye by the drink or by the bottle.

The proprietor was Adam Bush. He and his two sons ran the store. They were happy to get news from the east. Adam told them that he had heard that the army was looking for a location to establish a fort, to offer protection for wagon trains.

Oli met with Mr. Bush and offered to trade his potatoes for some used saddle bags. They would work well if, or when, he found the gold. Adam looked over the potatoes.

"You know, I could get these in the ground and have taters for the winter," Adam decided. He went and got the well-worn saddlebags for Oli.

Oli could spare the potatoes. He no longer worried about food. He had a good supply of jerked meat. The jerked meat lasted well in the dry climate they now traveled in.

The wagon that Oli was driving developed a dry wheel spindle after they left the trading post. The sun was at high noon. Pulling the team over to the side of the trail, Oli allowed the other wagons to pass. Jack Alberts rode back to see what the problem was. He offered to hold the train up for him.

"No, Jack, It won't take long to lube it. I will hurry the team along after finishing and should catch up before you camp for the night."

"Alright, Oli. Make sure you keep an eye on the horizon. If you see any Indians, cut the wagon loose and ride the team back to the train. I don't want to lose your rifle, or you."

As Jack turned away, Oli looked up and grinned. "Don't you worry, Jack. I'll be right along. Could you take the good horse with you, just in case?"

Nodding, Jack rode to the back of the wagon, and headed back to the train leading Oli's good horse.

Propping a block against the axle, Oli moved the team forward. This lifted the noisy wheel off the ground. Oli quickly lubed the spindle and installed the wheel. He made a mental note to check the rest of the wheels tonight. Putting everything away, Oli climbed up into the seat.

He could see the wagon train a couple of miles ahead. Starting the team after the train, Oli noticed something dark south of him. Standing, he continued to look as the team moved at a fast walk. As Oli's wagon moved up a gentle prairie swell, the dark objects became clear. Indians!

He counted eight mounted braves watching his movements. They were about one mile away and walking their horses parallel to Oli's path. As the prairie dipped the braves disappeared.

Oli felt a chill run down his spine. Urging the team to a trot, he closed on the wagon train. He strained his eyes to get another glimpse of the Indians. Was there a depression in the prairie that would allow them to close in on the lone wagon before he caught up?

He positioned his rifle for easier access. He could feel the heat of the afternoon sun. Puffs of dust rose with each step of the horses. Heat waves obscured the prairie, making it difficult to see the horizon. There was sweat dripping under his shirt and, with his heart pounding, Oli slowly closed on the others.

Seeing Oli hurrying, Jack pulled the lead wagon off the trail. "Circle the wagons! Keep the stock inside the circle. I want every gun charged and ready. We need every man scanning the horizon for trouble!" Jack shouted.

Oli pulled his wagon into a gap left for him. Leaping down, he unhooked the team and led them to the others. The ladies rushed up to strip the harness off his team. Oli ran to report to Jack.

"I spotted eight mounted braves pacing me about a mile out on the prairie."

The group spent the afternoon watching the horizon as the sun slowly slid down in the western sky. Oli watched as Jack worked his way around the wagons. He stopped beside Oli.

"Do you think Bart is okay?" Oli asked.

"I don't expect to see Bart until after dark. He won't expose himself until it is safe to come in," Jack replied. "I don't think we have any immediate worries, Oli. My guess is it was a scouting party. They will check our strength and how we react."

About an hour after sunset, Bart came in. Jack called the men together. "Bart what did you find there?"

Sipping on a cup of barely warm coffee, Bart took a deep breath. "The wagon train is being followed. Each day I see more tracks. Right now, I would estimate there are 40 to 50 Indians. They are Pawnee. I have seen signs of women and children traveling with them. They travel like a hunting party.

My guess is they are looking at us as an unexpected opportunity. They are trying to decide if they should attack, or just try to steal at night. If they can attack and scatter us, they will be able to grab what they can and go."

Jack turned to the men. "You heard Bart's opinion. If they were a raiding party, the Pawnee would have struck as soon as they spotted us. If we are to survive, we need to be disciplined. An attack can be expected when we are strung out and can be divided. Oli was lucky today. The Indians were not ready to show their hand. From now on, we will vary the time we leave in the morning. It will prevent a pattern. We will be stopping two to three hours before dark, depending on when we find a good spot for defending. The cook fire will be burnt down to coals by sunset. The most important thing is to keep close."

Jack then assigned the men to a watch schedule. Oli pulled an early watch and took his position. The stars filled the clear night sky. A soft breeze was blowing, bringing in the fragrance of the wild flowers and removing the heat of the day. He strained to hear all the night sounds. He could hear the wolves that followed the buffalo herd, howling to each other. Night birds and crickets competed to fill the air with sound. There was soft conversation coming from some of the wagons. No doubt the men were trying to re-assure their families.

The wagon train continued to stay on high alert, varying their schedule and staying close.

Jack stopped Oli one morning. "We are in need of fresh meat. We have not seen any Indian activity for a couple days. I have been hearing turkeys the past couple of days. Why don't you go out and see if you can get some?"

"Be happy to, Jack. I won't range too far. Young Michael can drive the wagon." Oli started to turn to get Michael.

"Just a minute, Oli, stick this in your belt in case. Fire two quick shots if you get in trouble." Jack handed Oli his spare cap and ball revolver.

With the handgun safely tucked in his belt and his Kentucky long rifle cradled in his arm, Oli walked off to find some game. He went about three-quarters of a mile from the train, slowly moving along a creek bottom.

He could hear some turkeys ahead. Crouching down and moving carefully, Oli was making sure that he didn't step on any twigs. Inching over the edge of the bank, he could see the wagon train moving to his right. His rifle was charged with birdshot. Rising a bit more, Oli froze.

Not a hundred yards ahead of him were a dozen braves, ready to attack. They were communicating with another group. Oli realized that this was the source of the turkey sounds.

Oli looked at the wagon train. It was about to enter a narrow and rough area that would prevent maneuvering, and would most likely string them out. Oli realized that if he fired he would give away his position, but if he did not the wagon train might be lost.

Raising the revolver into the air Oli fired twice and began to run, angling toward the wagon train. Startled, the Pawnees leaped forward, letting out curdling screams and commencing the attack. Oli could only guess that they did not realize where the shots came from.

The wagon train immediately started pulling into a circle. Oli could hear Jack shouting out orders. Just as the wagons closed the circle and began to try and get the horses in, the Pawnees swept down, riding in a wide circle around the wagons.

The wagon train abandoned their efforts to get all the horses and oxen in. Return fire started from the wagons. The Pawnees rode low, some shooting arrows from under their horse's necks. Oli continued to run toward the wagons. He could see flames rising from Wink's wagon. Wink was lying under the wagon firing while Eve loaded his rifles.

Oli saw stock falling as arrows struck them. Now running blindly toward the fight, he had the revolver in one hand and his rifle in the other. His foot hit a depression and he fell headlong, filling his mouth with dirt. Spitting to clear his mouth, Oli forced himself to think.

Frenchy's words came back to him. He didn't hesitate, and did react. The handgun lay on the ground about four feet in front of him. Oli still had his rifle. He brought up the rifle and drew a bead on one of the braves.

His shot was on target, but it was birdshot. The brave yelled out and fell from his horse. He leaped up, blood streaming from several holes in his back, and ran toward an opening between two wagons. A rifle sounded from inside the wagons and spun the Pawnee. He landed on his back with an ugly gash across his chest.

Crawling forward, Oli grabbed and lifted the revolver. He knew that the Pawnees were out of range, but he hoped to confuse them. Oli fired three spaced shots. He could hear firing coming from his left.

The braves suddenly broke, and it was over as quickly as it had started. They scooped up the dead or wounded as they retreated. The firing stopped from the wagon train. Oli had his rifle reloaded. He was unable to load the cap and ball gun.

Oli knew that Bart was out there someplace. Another shot sounded to his left. Stuffing the handgun into his belt, he began to run in the direction of the firing. About a quarter of a mile in front of the circled wagons, Oli found Bart.

He was down in a buffalo wallow with his leg pinned under his dead horse. The broken shaft of an arrow stuck out of his shoulder. Two braves were circling, looking for an opportunity to send another arrow into Bart. Oli drew down on the closest brave and squeezed off a shot. The ball cut a deep crease across the brave's shoulder blades, knocking him down. Before Oli could reload his rifle, the two Pawnees disappeared.

With his rifle loaded, Oli leaped into the wallow. Digging dirt away from Bart's leg and prying the carcass with his long rifle, he was able to free him from under the lifeless horse. Bart collapsed onto his back. His face was twisted with pain and Oli gasped when he saw the leg. His heel was to the front. Looking around quickly, Oli couldn't see any more Pawnees.

"Bart, I'll get something to support the leg. You keep any Indians away with your revolver."

Bart grimaced, sweat running down his face as he adjusted the leg. "The gun is empty, Oli. If you had not come, I would have been as dead as this horse shortly."

Oli found a couple of acceptable sticks and returned to Bart. Digging some leather strings from Bart's saddle bags, Oli did his best to set the leg and splint it. They were in luck. It did appear to be a clean break and had not broken the skin. Looking at the arrow in Bart's shoulder, Oli decided that he'd better not tackle that.

Getting Bart to his feet, Oli supported Bart's arm over his shoulder and they began to move toward the wagons. As soon as they became visible from the wagons, Oli heard a shout and saw Wink running towards them. With Wink's help they got Bart back to the wagon train.

Making him comfortable on a blanket, Oli looked up and saw Mrs. Weber rushing toward them. She had a pail of hot water and some clean white cloth.

"Step back and let me get to this man. Someone get me some more hot water!" she shouted over her shoulder.

Oli watched in awe as Mrs. Weber quickly and quite professionally removed the broken arrow shaft and started cleaning the wound. Young Michael came up with more hot water and knelt to assist Mrs. Weber as she fashioned a bandage on Bart.

Looking around, Oli saw the area in disarray. Harnesses lay everywhere, boxes of goods had been tossed down to fortify their defenses. A fire for treating the wounded had been started in the center.

Oli could see Wink's wagon pulled away from the circle, still smoldering. The downed animals were being dragged away from the wagons. Oli was surprised to find out that none of the downed animals had been killed by arrows. Jack was forced to shoot some of the animals in their harnesses to prevent them from stampeding and pulling the wagon out of position.

Evidently, the Pawnee had hoped to get the horses and hadn't wanted to kill them. Oli watched as two men butchered one of the downed oxen. Oli moved around the wagons, trying to assist in getting things back in order. Shortly, everything was sorted out and stowed.

Mrs. Weber came up to him. "Sit down, Oli. I got to take care of your face."

"My face?" Oli was surprised. He had not realized that when he'd fallen, his forehead, nose and chin had been severely scraped.

"Where did you learn doctoring?" Oli asked.

"Keep still, young man. I worked for a country doctor back east. Many a time when he was gone it was my job to fix folks up. Just wish I had some of the tools from there. I could do a better job."

Oli was impressed with the tenderness of her cleaning.

"You did a good job on Bart's leg. It should heal fine." Finishing up on his face, Mrs. Weber placed her hand momentarily on Oli's shoulder, then rushed off to see if anyone else needed help. Oli found Jack sitting with Bart.

Bart was telling him what had happened. "Like I said, I heard the two shots and started back toward the train. The Pawnees figured I would do this and were waiting for me. The two coming at me were between me and the wagon train. I pulled the horse into a wallow just as the arrows hit him. Down he went, pinning my leg. With it broken, I couldn't pull it out. Then riding by, they got the arrow into my shoulder. I tried to pull it out and it broke off. I got my revolver and rifle out. I kept them off with an occasional shot. I had just fired the last one when Oli came up. I would have been deader than heck in short order if he had not driven them off."

Jack looked up at Oli. "Going to need you to scout until Bart can get back on his feet."

Oli flushed for a moment. "I am not a scout, Jack."

"Well, right now you are the closest we got to a scout. Bart can let you know what to watch for."

Nodding, Oli left the two and went over to see how the good horse was doing. Rubbing the horse's neck, Oli confided, "I fear they have more faith in me than I have."

He heard Wink call him. Walking over, Oli saw Wink and Eve standing next to the wagon he had been driving.

"My wagon is destroyed, Oli," Wink said. "Eve and I have to move back into her wagon. Not much was saved from my wagon, so we have room to keep your stuff."

Oli looked at the burnt wagon. "Sorry about your wagon and stuff. If you need anything from my packs, you are welcome to it. It was a good thing we brought the extra wagon, Wink. It will work out well. Jack wants me to do some scouting, so young Michael or Eve would have ended up driving anyway."

Eve stepped closer to Oli. "We will want you to join us each evening for supper and we can keep the good horse with us for you."

Slapping Oli on the back, Wink said, "Then it's settled."

With one less wagon and one of the Pawnee horses that had decided to stay near the wagon train stock, they were able to outfit all remaining wagons with a team. Jack kept the wagon train on high alert.

Oli reported to Jack for scouting duties. Bart had made some recommendations to him about keeping to low ground, taking care when he did have to climb a rise to look around, and what to look for in a good campsite. While Oli had surmised much of this already, he was courteous and listened to Bart's instructions.

He confided in Jack that he did not have a lot of riding experience. Jack gave him a large bay to ride. Jack assured him that the horse was tame and not easily spooked. Swinging up into the saddle and having Jack's extra revolver tucked in his belt, Oli moved out, cradling the Kentucky long rifle in the crook of his arm. It felt good to be up in the saddle.

Oli walked the horse past the buffalo wallow where he had found Bart. When the men went back after the attack, they had found the animal stripped of anything of value, and the hind quarters cut off and taken. Oli could see the rotting, legless carcass.

"Darn waste of good horse flesh," he muttered.

Looking over the prairie, Oli noticed that the grass was getting brown and goldenrod was in bloom. He kept to low ground, riding up the slopes just enough to see the horizon. Jack had told him that it would be unlikely that the Pawnee would come back. They would now be busy hunting buffalo meat for the winter. Taking off the horse's hindquarters proved that the Indians were short on food. Oli knew that horse flesh was okay to eat, but he would not choose it over whitetail or buffalo.

For the next six weeks, Oli enjoyed the job of scouting. Riding out alone each morning with the late summer breeze in his face and the warm sun on his back was exhilarating. Each day he saw new country. At a glance it looked like just more prairie, but to the trained eye, which he now had, it looked as different as one person's face to another.

Riding out early one morning, Oli spotted something out on the prairie southwest of the wagon train. He worked the bay in that direction, making sure to scan the horizon around the trail. The object slowly took shape.

It was a wagon, or what was left of a wagon. Riding up, Oli could see the bleached bones of horses scattered around the area. Evidence showed that the horrific scene was from the previous year. The wagon had been burnt and some pieces of furniture lay in the prairie grass behind the wagon.

Oli pulled the bay up when he spotted four neat mounds of earth. The two in the center were much shorter than the outside mounds. Dismounting, he walked up to the graves. Oli knelt briefly at the graves and said a prayer. He swung back into the saddle and let the bay have its head for a while as he thought about the family in the unmarked graves. A family, with hopes and dreams of building a home in the West, had perished on the windblown prairie.

Often, Oli was able to bring back some game, be it a deer or various birds. It was a thrill when he first saw the mountains appear on the horizon. Each day they were a little bigger. They were now about two days out from where Oli would go his way, and the wagon train would go theirs.

Bart was starting to get around pretty good. "I'll be able to take over the scouting when we get to where we split up," he told Oli.

Oli smiled at Bart. "I'll miss riding the bay."

Bart shifted uncomfortably. "I got to tell you something, Oli. It was me who stole your boots."

"I know, Bart, and it was me who stole them back," Oli confided.

Looking at Oli's boots, and then his face, Bart got a sheepish look. "They do look familiar. I am sorry I took them. When I drink I tend to do things I am not proud of."

Smiling and extending his hand, Bart said, "I am glad it was you who got them."

CHAPTER SEVEN

Oli sat watching the wagon train slowly move out of sight. Wink's wagon was last, and Oli could see young Michael and the two girls waving over and over as the wagon lumbered on. The good horse nuzzled his shoulder. Rubbing the side of the horse's neck, Oli thought about the morning.

That morning, Oli had woke up with just a bit of a headache. He had shared a little whiskey with some of the men as a farewell party. After a couple cups of strong hot coffee, Oli's head had cleared.

Wink had been waiting for Oli near the wagon. "You ready for the final test, Oli?"

His friend had placed a piece of plank against a log. The two men had stood about 25 feet away.

Eve raised her hand. "Now!"

Both men's arms had flashed, grabbing their knives and throwing. Wink's blade had reached the plank a split second before Oli's.

"By golly, Oli, I thought you had me beat for a second. You have become a damn good man with a knife."

Oli had puffed up. Wink had a way of even making a loss sound like a form of victory.

Mrs. Weber had walked by. "Your face healed up nicely, Oli."

Oli had glanced at the three dirty-faced children following her and couldn't help smiling. "I owe the good results to your care, Mrs. Weber."

"Yep," Mrs. Weber had replied, and continued on to the fire.

Jack had come by and brought Oli a small package. "Some extra ball, flint, and powder for you to make up for what you used to keep us in meat."

Looking around, Jack had asked, "When is your friend supposed to meet you?"

Oli had looked up and down the river. "I would have expected him to be here already. I am sure he will be along soon. I'll set up camp here and wait."

He'd also received a surprising visit from Bart. "I have a couple things you might find handy. From here on you won't have a water barrel handy," Bart had told him.

Bart had handed Oli an army issued canteen and a crisply folded neckerchief. Bart had then given Oli a quick salute, before he swung into the saddle and rode out ahead of the train.

Oli sat as the last sound of the wagon train disappeared. All he could hear was the crunching as the good horse pulled at the prairie grass, birds singing in the cottonwoods, and a far off screech of a hawk or eagle. It was a beautiful late August day. It was time to take stock. Oli opened the package Jack had given him. Sitting on top of the musket balls was a shiny $20 gold piece.

Oli looked toward where the wagons had gone. "Thank you, Jack." Opening up his ledger, Oli took inventory.

2 wool shirts, 1 wool pants, 2 pair woolen socks, 1 long underwear, 1 pair boots. 1 darning, needle, 1 leather awl, 1 whetstone, 1 knife, 1 razor, 6 leather strings, 1 wool blanket, 1 deerskin coat, 1 fine hat, 1 belt, 1 ground canvas, 1 tent, 2 flints, 1 coffee pot, 1 cook pot, 4 fish hooks, 1 neckerchief, 1 Kentucky long rifle, 1 possible bag, 1 powder horn, powder, ball, oil, patches, 2 canteens, 1 good horse with bridle, 1 pack rig, 1 pair of saddle bags, 1 mess kit (cup, plate, bowl, spoon)

"Well," Oli told the good horse, "I have been better off, but I still have enough to search for the gold. I used the last of the leather to put soles on the boots. They should last me a while."

Putting the pack rig on the good horse, Oli split the packs between himself and the horse. The good horse was carrying about 150 pounds and Oli's pack was 100 pounds. Kicking dirt over his small noon fire, he took the map out of the coat lining and took a long look at it. Securing it back under the lining, he rolled the coat up and tied it to the good horse's pack. With that, Oli headed north.

It was hot on the high desert, dirt devils swirled by in the afternoon breeze. Keeping the mountains to his left, Oli walked, feeling the dry ground crunch under his feet. Tumbleweeds rolled by, spreading their seeds for next year.

Wiping the sweat from his face with the back of his sleeve, Oli scanned the horizon. He tilted the canteen to his lips, taking a drink of the warm, less than satisfying water. Smiling, he looked down at the canteen. You could never know a guy from first impressions. He continued walking, with the good horse following obediently.

First impressions sure could be wrong. Bart Nevell was a big bruiser, but a big bruiser you could depend on; that is, unless he was drinking. Now, Mrs. Weber, she had three cute, if not clean, little ones and a shiftless husband. She needed to keep the kids fed. When it came to a fight, she was the first one you wanted around if you were wounded.

If one lived with first impressions only, they would want to keep distance from both of those folks. If one took the time to know them a bit better, they were the types to keep close.

Oli stopped in the middle of a step with his skin crawling. He could hear the sounds of turkeys. His eyes searched for the source of noise. Pawnees, or turkeys?

"Let them be turkeys," he whispered.

Dropping the lead rope of the good horse, Oli crept up the knoll, clutching his long rifle. Relief spread over him when he saw the flock of 12 turkeys busy eating grasshoppers from the switch grass.

Double checking the surrounding hills for any dangers, he focused on a nice fat turkey. He wanted a head shot, to minimize damage to the meat. Oli lined up and squeezed the trigger. He continued on his way with supper hanging from his belt.

He found a grove of aspen with water nearby and set up camp for the night. While plucking the turkey he estimated the amount of time it would take to get into the gold area. He had talked with Jack about what was north of the Platte River.

Jack had drawn the layout in the dirt with a stick. One of the rivers he'd mentioned was the Stinking Water River. Jack had said it flowed into the Big Horn and on to the Yellowstone. It had sounded right to Oli. Based on the map, he was 22 days walk from the gold.

Laughing, Oli looked at the good horse grazing to his right. "That is, if there is even any gold to be found."

Staring up at the heavens, Oli shouted, "What have you gotten me into, Jolly!"

Sitting in his tent, cross-legged on his blanket, Oli sipped a cup of coffee. His fire was down to red coals. Oli was making sure he did not look at the fire or coals. He loved the night sky, he had the feeling that if he reached out he could pluck a star out of the heavens.

Captain Jacob had shown him how to navigate using the stars. Oli looked up and wondered if the *Gustav* had gotten back to Finland. Were they heading back now, and could they be looking at the same stars as he was?

Wolves started howling. They were joined by some coyotes that must have been closing in on an unfortunate rabbit or other game. Their yelps became louder and closer together. Bull frogs were croaking, crickets were chirping. Oli stared out at the dark. He had a feeling that he had not had since he'd left the farm in Finland. He was alone, all alone.

If he slipped and hurt himself, there was no one to help. Oli's thoughts went back to the wagon with the windblown graves. His stomach began to get queasy. He heard the soft snort of the good horse. The familiar sound was comforting. He would never be alone as long as he had the good horse.

Oli woke to a bright, clear dawn. He hurriedly made his morning fire, anxious to shake off the night's chill. After a quick breakfast of weak coffee and biscuits, he broke camp. Once he had carefully looked around, Oli left the security of the aspen and led the good horse towards the distant foothills.

With the sun high in the sky, he stopped to rest himself and the good horse. He sat on the south side of a rise and was enjoying a soft breeze. He could see a hawk sitting on a lonely dead tree. Suddenly, it swooped down upon an unsuspecting prey. Clutching its catch in its sharp claws, the hawk looked around before taking off with the rabbit, which was kicking its last.

Fascinated by the hawk, Oli almost missed the distant voices. There were men talking on the other side of the rise. Straining his ears, he was unable to tell if it was white men or Indians. Slowly, Oli crawled to the top of the rise and looked into a valley with a dried creek bed running through it.

He could see three men sitting across the valley, busy making a noonday meal. Their horses were tied to low brush along the creek. The men appeared to be trappers, or maybe hunters, heading for the mountains. Oli was about to turn back to get the good horse and head down to introduce himself when a slight movement caught the corner of his eye.

Carefully, Oli scanned the valley. Then he saw the horses tied in a clump of trees about one hundred yards from him. The movement he had seen was when one of them had swished its tail at a fly. The horses had Indian rigs on them. Oli felt his stomach tighten. Were the Indians after him, or the men below?

Retrieving the long rifle and powder horn from the good horse, Oli moved back up to the top of the rise. He felt naked lying there without any cover. He tried to flatten himself as much as possible against the ground. Removing his hat, he peered through the sparse grass. He stared, afraid to blink for fear of missing some movement. Oli's eyes stung and began to tear. Forced to blink the tears away, he finally picked out one of the braves below.

Relief washed over him as he realized that they were after the other men and not him. The relief was short-lived. He had counted six horses, which meant that there were five more Indians crawling towards the unsuspecting men. He couldn't let this happen, yet he did not want them to come after him.

He had only a muzzle loader and would not be able to fire very many shots if they changed their objective. For all he knew, one of the other five might be close to him. Movement near the men caught Oli's attention. One of the Indians was about a hundred feet from the camp. Oli made his decision.

A 100 yard shot at the horses would require a steady hand. While the long rifle had superior accuracy over other muzzle loaders, the horses were near the end of its range. The Indians were further yet and definitely out of range. Aiming above the backs of the horses, Oli squeezed off a shot. The long rifle was loud in the midday stillness.

He must have scored a hit somewhere amongst the horses. They began kicking and bucking, pulling themselves loose from the tethers, their shrill whinnies splitting the air.

The men in the camp were laying low with rifles in their hands, trying to figure out where the shot came from. The closest Indian leaped up and with a war cry charged the men. A shot from one the men cut him down in mid-stride.

Oli watched the other Indians running back to round up their horses. The three men grabbed their mounts and pack animals and headed out in the opposite direction. Before they disappeared one of the trappers, a tall, thin man carrying a Hawken .50, looked back wondering where the shot came from that had alerted them.

Oli wasted no time. Scrambling down to the good horse, he moved back into the valley and headed for the distant cover of some wooded hills. Reaching the safety of the trees, the reality of what had just happened struck him and his legs began to shake. He sank down at the base of a windblown oak. He had saved the men, but had he endangered himself. Would the Indians decide to track him?

He stuck to the foothills of the mountains for safety, as he worked his way north. The elevation of the hills gave him a much better range of vision. He would be able to see movement out on the prairie while it was difficult to see him. It also gave him a better vantage to see landmarks from the map.

CHAPTER EIGHT

Seven days into the trek north, Oli stopped and stared in awe. It was about high noon and he was looking into the most beautiful valley he had ever laid eyes on. The opening was about 200 yards wide. The valley extended back about two miles. There was an eight acre pond on the north side that was supplied by a fifty foot waterfall cascading down the sheer rock wall. The south side was made up of rolling hills covered with timber. The valley was carpeted in lush, green grass dotted with late summer flowers.

Oli walked into the valley and stopped by the pond. The water was clear and cold. He took a long, satisfying drink. "You know, good horse, we may have just found heaven."

The good horse was listening to Oli with one ear while busily pulling on the plentiful grass. There was a small grove of cedar on the east side of the pond. Oli set camp up among them. The pungent smell of their evergreen branches reminded him of a grove he had played in as a young boy.

He rubbed the good horse down with large handfuls of cedar foliage. Smiling, he figured that the horse would smell great. He then picketed the good horse a short distance from his camp. A fire was started with dry branches from the cedar trees. It snapped loudly, sending off showers of sparks. Oli closed his eyes, enjoying the fragrance of the cedar wood smoke. He then added some wood from a nearby oak tree.

With the fire going well, he got out a fish hook and line. Securing these to a pole, he put on a worm found under a rotting log, and set about fishing. In less than 30 minutes, Oli had ten nice largemouth bass.

Glancing at the sky, he estimated that there was about two hours before sunset and he was very hungry, so he decided to eat some fresh-broiled fish before setting up the tent. Putting the coffee water on first, Oli then skewered three of the fish on green branches and propped them over the fire to cook. Sitting back against a tree, Oli was enjoying the aroma of fish broiling and boiling coffee.

"Hello, the camp!" Oli jumped up upon hearing the voice.

Looking towards the opening of the valley, he saw what could only be a crusty old trapper, riding on a crow-bait horse and leading a pack horse that wasn't any better. The trapper was stoop-shouldered, sporting a long beard, and covered his head with a wide, floppy hat. He had a buckskin shirt with tattered fringes on the sleeves.

"My name's Jed. I saw the fire and hoped you had some coffee on."

Oli waved him over. "Come on in. I'm Oli, I have a pot of coffee and plenty of fish."

Oli couldn't believe how happy he was to see another human. He had only been alone less than two weeks and it seemed like forever. Oli put the second brace of fish on to broil and felt that he was chattering like a magpie. He told Jed about the Indians and three men, about the wagon train, and St. Louis. He just could not help himself. With only the good horse to talk to and getting no answers back, it felt good talking to Jed.

Looking at the rifle beside Jed, Oli asked, "Is that a .50 or .54 caliber Hawken?"

"It's a .50 caliber," Jed responded, patting the rifle.

Drinking good, strong brew, and waiting for the next helping of fish to cook, Oli asked Jed where he was bound for.

"I'll be heading east from here. I have some friends that have been buffalo hunting. Plan to join up with them and go south this winter. You think those fish are done?"

Oli turned to look. There was a burst of light and everything went dark.

* * *

The redheaded woman came close to Oli. She pushed her damp, cold face against his. "I'll get us some more to drink, Oli."

He watched her remove money from his money belt. "That's too much," Oli complained.

Shaking her red hair, she came back over to him. Once again she pressed her cold damp face against . . . Oli opened his eyes and looked into the brown eyes of the good horse. The horse had been nuzzling him. Why? It was first light!

Oli started to get up when the world began to spin. He collapsed back onto the ground. His head was throbbing. He began to retch. With each heave his head pounded harder. In agony, Oli cried out. Everything went dark again.

He was on a boat, someone was chasing him, could it be Indians? He kept falling, he needed to get up but things were spinning. He had to go, had to get off the boat.

He opened his eyes. The sun was high in the sky. From where he lay he could see the good horse grazing. Slowly, he started to get up. The head still throbbed, but if he moved slowly the spinning stopped. Oli's eyes did not want to focus. Blinking rapidly, he sat there with his head hanging. He could smell vomit. What had happened? Oli felt the blood-crusted hair on the back of his head. He also felt the shaft of his good knife still in its sheath.

Taking care to keep his head level, he slowly turned his shoulders and looked around. His packs were gone. Also his coat with the map! Oli slowly moved to the tree and carefully sat against it. The long rifle was missing. So was the coffee pot.

Oli slowly became aware that he had wet himself while lying unconscious. He wanted to cry. His face was covered with vomit, his pants were damp with urine, and all of his stuff was gone.

Fighting down the urge to panic, he scolded himself. "You have to think. It is your only hope."

Unable to stand, Oli dragged himself to the pond. Removing his soiled pants and underwear, he slid into the cold water. With shaky movements, he washed the vomit off his face. Suddenly realizing how dry his mouth was, he swirled the dirty water away. Oli scooped up some water and rinsed his mouth, swallowing a small amount. Sliding back to the edge of the water he slowly rinsed the pants and underwear.

Once out of the water, the sun's warmth quickly stopped Oli from shaking. He draped his clothing over some bushes. Then, exhausted, he collapsed onto the grass next to the pond. His eyes opened again. He must have passed out. The constant throb continued in his head.

Oli sat up and looked at his nakedness. His side that was exposed to the sun was slightly burned. He groaned, realizing that he had one more thing that would hurt. The sun was low in the sky. He sat trying to focus, waiting for the ache in his head to subside. He could see some elk feeding in the valley. He wished that life could be that simple. A shiver went through Oli. It was cooling off. Painfully, he dressed.

Oli then realized that the money belt was gone. "Damn!" he exclaimed.

With his clothes back on, he looked around. He could see the good horse cropping grass. Why hadn't Jed taken the good horse? He noticed that the bridle was off. Jed had released the horse. That meant he'd thought that Oli was dead. Jed had seen no value in the horse, but hadn't wanted it left picketed or dragging a picket rope.

He snorted, "He thought more of a horse than me."

Oli suddenly remembered that he had left the pot and fishing pole down by the pond. Crawling along the edge of the pond, he paused several times until the feeling of nausea passed. He finally located the items. Drinking a bit more water, he then filled the pot with water. Dragging the pot along the ground, he headed back toward the fire pit, splashing water with each move.

Taking a piece of flint from his pocket, Oli showered sparks onto some tinder. Once he had the fire going, he put the pot next to it. He leaned against the tree. The rough bark hurt his bruised head. After a little adjusting, he was able to sit back. He must have dozed.

When Oli opened his eyes, it was dark and the coals were glowing red. He could see steam coming out of the pot. Moving to the fire, he sipped some of the hot water. It made him feel better. He dipped the end of his neckerchief into the hot water and started bathing the back of his head. Each touch stung hard enough to bring tears to Oli's eyes. He knew that he had to clean the scalp to prevent infection. He added wood to the fire and emptied the bloody water.

Using a makeshift walking stick, he pushed himself to his feet. Oli stood swaying for a moment. He noticed that the small effort of standing had brought sweat to his brow. Holding the pot in one hand and the walking stick in the other, he slowly went back to the pond and got fresh water. Once it was warm, he drank more of the water. Exhausted, he pulled some loose cedar boughs over him for warmth, and curled up under the trees.

Oli woke up shivering from head to toe. His head still ached and the sunburn felt tight and stung. While the days were warm on the high desert, the nights were cold. The sun was just coming up, providing a wide swath of light through the opening of the valley.

With teeth chattering and hands shaking, Oli struggled to get a fire going. Once he had a few flames, he fed them dead cedar branches. The cedar quickly caught fire, snapping and crackling. Oli curled up into a ball next to the fire, smoke bathing his chilled body. With more effort than Oli thought it should take, he moved the pot of water next to the fire and sat up, looking around.

The good horse was gone. The consequences of being without a horse did not settle in right away. Oli's stomach was burning with hunger. Slowly, he moved down to the pond with some earthworms wiggling in his hand. Sitting on the bank with his aching head hanging, Oli held the fishing pole and waited for a hungry bass to find the worm.

Once again, it didn't take long before Oli had two fat fish. He stumbled back to the fire and put the bass on sticks that Jed had left lying on the ground after stripping the fish off them. Oli did not even bother to clean the fish. He just stuck the sticks in their mouth and began broiling them.

The water began to steam in the pot. Oli took the first fish off the fire. It was barely done. The fish tasted better than Oli had ever remembered fish tasting. Sipping hot water and munching on the fish, Oli rapidly started to feel better. The warm sun on his back and the fire's warmth in front, he was almost feeling hope again.

Oli spent the morning eating fish, sipping warm water, and tenderly cleaning the cut on the back of his head. While still weak, he felt less shaky.

"He must have hit me with the damn Hawken barrel," Oli mumbled.

Standing and using an improvised walking stick he'd made from an oak branch, Oli moved out into the valley. Quickly tired, he sat in the tall grass. Plucking a blade of grass, he chewed on the tender stem and searched the valley. The elk were still on the far end, grazing peacefully.

In his weakened condition and without a horse, he was unable to figure out how he could go after Jed. Every day that passed put Jed and the map farther away. Painfully, Oli stood and waited for the throbbing in his skull to subside a bit. Even walking slowly was exhausting. On weak legs, he continued across the valley. He noticed something along the edge of the hills.

Relief flooded over him. It was the good horse near the edge of the timber. He called to the good horse with a weak voice. The animal looked up and saw Oli standing there. It whinnied and trotted towards him.

Oli had noticed the bridle lying near the picket pin. The good horse appeared quite happy to see Oli on his feet. Wrapping his fingers in the good horse's mane, the two of them moved toward the fire.

He spoke quietly to his horse. "What chance do we have finding Jed? An injured man and an old horse."

Realizing what he had said, Oli put his arms around the horse's neck. "I'm sorry, I meant to say, good horse, that you are a good friend and a good horse."

It took another day before he felt steady enough to start after Jed. He had found his ledger lying next to the tree where he had planned to set his tent up. The pack rig and a canteen also lay there, obviously overlooked by Jed. Oli opened it, grasped the short pencil and entered his assets.

1 wool shirt, 1 underwear, 1 wool pants, 1 pair socks, 1 pair boots, 1 belt, 1 hat, 1 neckerchief, 1 good horse, 1 bridle and lead rope, 1 pot, 1 canteen, 4 fish hooks, Good Knife and sheath, 1 flint, 10 fish dried

Oli started out with the sun just coming up. He was riding the good horse. While his head had stopped throbbing, he still tired quickly. He had his meager belongings. He used the neckerchief to secure the pot to his belt. The fish were in the pot with a cedar branch cover. He left the packing rig near the cedars, with intentions of coming back to pick it up. The good horse stepped out briskly, like he was happy to move on. Oli hugged the horse's neck to absorb some warmth.

At the mouth of the valley, Oli found Jed's tracks. He was thankful that there had been no rain to wash them out. It appeared that Jed was not worried about being followed. He'd made no attempt to cover his tracks.

"Yep, he figured I was dead," Oli said to the good horse.

Jed was heading east, following an unnamed stream, so Oli didn't have to worry about water. Just after noon, Oli came up to a cluster of wild plum bushes. The fruit was small, hard, and deep purple. The sun was high, with plenty of daylight left, so he stopped and ate some. The tart fruit was a welcome change to his diet of fish. After his immediate hunger was taken care of, he picked and added plums to the pot.

Returning to the good horse, Oli's legs began to cramp as he walked. He was riding without a saddle and clinging to the animals back with his legs. The task of holding on was taking its toll. Using a windfall, he climbed back onto the good horse.

Continuing to follow the trail, Oli found Jed's evening camp. It was easy to spot. Jed had gone through Oli's stuff, discarding items he hadn't wanted. Oli found the tent, a blanket, and ground tarp. His coffee pot had a hole shot through it. No doubt Jed had tested the long rifle. One of his empty packs also lay on the ground, next to his empty money belt.

Oli collected the things together and started a fire. Putting the pot next to the fire, he added some fish and plums to the water. He noticed some wild onions and added them to the pot. He knew it would not taste very good, but at least it would be hot and provide nourishment.

The next morning found him clinging to the good horse, his eyes fixed to the ground, following Jed's tracks. Even though Oli was tired, he knew that he had to keep riding. He had his few possessions tied in the pack behind him.

It was mid-afternoon when Oli saw buzzards circling ahead. Moving slowly, he could see where Jed had started his horses galloping. Shortly after, Oli saw tracks from five unshod ponies coming in from two sides at Jed's position.

Could they be the Indians he had surprised? Had they been tracking him and found Jed instead? Jed had released the pack horse and had continued to spur his horse ahead. Something reflecting the sun caught Oli's eye. It lay half-hidden by the bank next to the stream. It was his long rifle. Apparently, Jed had thrown it to lighten his load.

Oli picked it up and continued to follow the tracks. He stopped beside the spot where two Indians had caught the pack horse. The other three had continued to chase Jed. About a half mile beyond that, Oli found Jed and his horse.

He could see where the horse had collapsed, throwing Jed. Oli gasped as he looked at Jed's mutilated body. Flies buzzed loudly around him. He was staked to the ground and had been stripped naked. They had scalped him, and his beard had been removed with part of his chin. The body was a series of cuts. He had been blinded and then left to slowly die.

Oli felt ill as he looked at Jed. While he despised the man, and what he had done, Oli did not wish this type of death on anyone. The smell of his decaying body was strong. He cut Jed loose, moving the arms next to his sides, and started stacking rocks to cover the body.

He worked quietly, watching the area around him for any movement. The good horse was a good sentry. On the trail, Oli had noticed that the horse had excellent senses and would let him know if someone or something was coming. Standing over the makeshift grave, Oli prayed for Jed's crooked soul. Just maybe the way he died would atone for some of his mistakes in life.

He stepped back and looked over the scene. His heart jumped. He saw something under the dead horse. Struggling to dig out the stuff under the stiffened, bloated carcass, Oli found a pack crushed under the animal.

Sitting next to the animal, his finger nails torn and bleeding, he looked at the item. It was the pack with his deerskin coat. The pack was not used for bigger items, but did have his awl, needle, a shirt, his razor, a spare flint, his mess kit, and the small package from Jack containing some musket balls, patch, and powder.

Carefully looking around the area, Oli found a few coins. He put these into his money belt. They totaled $3.40. He also found some spilt coffee beans, which he carefully scooped up. Oli removed the saddle from Jed's horse and placed it onto the back of the good horse. Then he put the items he found together, and led the good horse back up the trail to about where the Indians had taken after Jed.

He made camp in a small grove of cottonwood. Bringing water to boil in the cook pot, Oli poured some of Jed's coffee in. The aroma almost made him forget about what he had seen today. Drinking the hot liquid, Oli chewed on a piece of fish.

He figured the shot Jed had taken at the coffee pot would have alerted the Indians to his presence. With that thought, Oli realized that every time he had to shoot game to survive, the sound of the shot could cause his death.

He decided that he would go back to the valley for a couple days to build up his strength. He would catch and smoke fish while the good horse enjoyed the green grass. He would then continue looking for the gold.

Oli spent four days in the valley. He sorted his supplies and repaired items as necessary. He took the opportunity to improve the pack rig, using items from Jed's saddle. He had one day of cold rain. He sat under the tent watching the rainfall and wind move the expanse of grass. It reminded him of the swells during the ocean crossing. The valley was beautiful. It offered seclusion and closed off the rest of the world. Oli knew that if he lived to be 100 years old, he would never find a better place to start a farm. Circumstances would not allow this. If the rain stopped tomorrow, he would have to leave. More than likely, he would never return.

CHAPTER NINE

One day blended into another. It seemed like he had been walking forever. Each morning, Oli woke to frost. He would huddle around his small fire, trying to gain warmth while heating his water. By midday the sun was hot and the air smelled of dust. Evening brought back the chill. He was in the high desert, and the day's heat was quickly lost.

As leaves turned brilliant colors, a cold breeze started blowing down from the mountains. Oli knew that he might be in trouble with the weather. He would never be able to survive a winter in the high elevation.

It was sunset when Oli came to a river. He guessed that it was the Stinking Water River. He had smelled it for the last few miles. The water had a sulfur-like odor, but was cold and clear.

Studying the map, he looked at the area around him. If he could not find the gold quickly, he would have to walk east and look for someplace to spend the winter. Oli had traveled carefully and kept his cook fires small since running into the Indians and finding Jed's body. He knew that there were Cheyenne around, and was doing everything possible not to draw attention.

Oli knew that his supplies were running low. He chose a camp under an overhang of rock. He had a wide view of the grass-covered prairie below. The cold nights had turned the grass a golden brown. Oli could see an occasional evergreen tree. The dark green was a sharp contrast to the grass. He hoped to spot an opportunity for food.

The next morning, the sunrise was a flaming orange sky. The wind was blowing and there was a haze across the prairie. He almost missed seeing one of the dark patches move. At this distance he could not tell if it was an elk or buffalo.

He made his way along a valley parallel to the one the animal was in. Slowly, Oli moved over the crest of the hill, pressing himself into the golden brown grass. It was a buffalo calf. He did not want to have to shoot more than once. Taking careful aim just behind the shoulder, Oli let his breath out and squeezed the trigger. The calf lurched forward and collapsed.

Oli's heart pounded all the while he butchered it, praying that his shot wasn't heard. He knew that on a cold, still, and clear morning, sound would travel for miles. The hazy, windy morning would help prevent that. He kept the hide for future warmth and wrapped the cuts of meat in it for the time being.

The good horse snorted and side stepped as Oli lifted the bloody package onto the pack rig. He moved his camp several miles before he dared stop. He needed to smoke and dry the extra meat. The hide also needed to be scraped.

Wrapped in his deerskin coat, he broiled buffalo steaks over the fire. Tonight, he would eat well. Tomorrow, he would start jerking the rest of the buffalo. It took two days to process the meat. Oli knew that he needed to keep looking for the gold, but to do that he would need food. With the new supplies packed on the good horse, he continued the quest.

Oli stood, searching the skyline. He absently chewed on some of the jerked meat. A blast of cold air made him pull the deerskin coat tighter around him to keep the wind out. He compared the mountain ridges with the map. The map had three crosses and a crescent between a double peak and a lower rounded peak.

He would move his camp up the mountain range for a day. The next day or two, he would walk south of the camp and then into the mountains, looking for landmarks that matched the map. He had started to leave the good horse in camp. If he did find gold, Oli wanted the good horse in good shape. He could walk 15 miles searching on a good day. Once Oli had an area searched, he would relocate the camp to a new area.

Moving deeper into the mountains and then back out to the foothills, the search was slow. Oli knew that he had only a matter of weeks left before early snows would drive him from the mountains. The sun was getting lower in the sky, the days shorter.

He was sitting and resting, while eating some beechnuts, when he noticed what looked like a faint trail leading into a rocky valley. He followed the trail for about a mile. Stopping, his heart began to pound.

In front of him were some low hills. The left was a double peak and to the right a rounded hill. Walking further into the valley, Oli noticed that the rock had some quartz. It appeared that he had entered a dead-end canyon.

Oli moved around the end of the canyon. It was about a mile wide. He could no longer see the hills. Moving back out of the canyon, he could again see the hills. To his right he could see a large, old, lightning-struck tree. Oli climbed the tree as high as was possible.

Slowly, he looked around the canyon. He could see an area with lines of quartz. The sun was getting close to setting and he was five miles from camp. He would have to go back and return tomorrow. He decided, tomorrow he would move his camp into the canyon. There was water and grass for the good horse.

Oli sat near his small cook fire and watched the water slowly come to a boil. He had a collection of items he had picked to put into the pot and make a soup. Wild onions were the main ingredient. He had also discovered some edible roots. He had noticed that animals were digging them up. He had tasted one and it had a musky, but pleasant, flavor. He also had jerky to add to the pot.

The canyon he'd gone into today gave him the most hope he'd had in a long time. The hills matched the map. It made sense that someone leaving the canyon would have looked back for a landmark to use to find it again. There was quartz. It was possible that from some angle it would make a crescent. Oli was sure that the crosses were the graves of those killed in the fight.

He only dared to hope that this was the end of the search. He was now working on borrowed time as far as the weather went. Sleep came hard that night. He was not able to shut his mind off. He now wished that he had spent a little more time in the canyon. And, of course, he worried that by some chance he would miss the faint trail leading back to the canyon.

It was late morning when Oli returned to the canyon. Resisting the urge to start searching immediately, he picketed the good horse on some thick grass, he put up his tent and set up his bedroll. He then took out the ledger and sketched the layout of the canyon.

This area was the most promising so far. The rest of the day was spent searching the canyon, taking care to keep the hills in view. That night Oli sat next to his fire, cooking jerky and onion soup. He had no coffee left. He missed it with his meals, especially in the morning.

The smell of winter was in the air. The tops of the mountains were white with snow. Leaves had already fallen from the trees at this elevation. That morning, Oli had found ice along the edge of the water. His time to search was growing short. Wood was not plentiful in the canyon, so Oli carried a pack with him and picked up any fuel he saw. He reached to grab a short stick as he walked. As his hand closed around it, he realized that it was not wood, but metal!

It was a rusted cutlass stuck into the ground. Oli felt a chill go through him. Someone had been in this canyon. Stepping back, he saw what appeared to be the ends of three mounds of stones. The cutlass was stuck into the ground at the end of one of the mounds. The dirt above the mounds had collapsed, almost covering them.

Could these mounds be the graves of the companions of the original owner of the map? Oli stared at the graves. Could the gold be buried in one of the graves? He sat on a rock, debating if he should dig in the mounds. It went against his values to disturb the resting place of the dead. But, if the gold had been buried in the graves of the dead Spaniards, it would be necessary.

Oli had realized some time back that he had neglected to bring a shovel. He had been afraid to look like a miner or treasure hunter, so he had stayed away from supplies that would give him away. He now thought that it hadn't been a good idea. Using his hands and the walking stick, Oli spent the rest of the day removing the rock and dirt off the mounds.

Tired, and covered with dust and sweat, Oli went back to camp to start supper. While he washed up, he decided that he would open the grave marked with the cutlass the next morning. Oli looked around the canyon and thought about what had happened here. There would have been a desperate battle fought for survival. The men would have seen their companions fall to the Indian arrows.

Oli did not sleep well that night. He dreamt of removing the stones from the grave and seeing the sightless eyes staring at him from the skull. The jaw moved . . . ! Oli awoke in a cold sweat. He pulled his blanket tighter around his neck. He knew that if he found the gold in a grave, he was not going to spend any additional time in this canyon.

He lay awake until the sun began to light the sky. He was sure that this canyon was haunted. Was the dream a warning? Oli was slow to make his breakfast. He was not anxious to go back to the graves. Finally, he could put it off no longer. Walking back to the grave site, Oli sat down. While the sun warmed the canyon, the chill going up and down his spine remained.

He decided that he would try and reason with the occupants' spirits before starting. Looking around, Oli's eyes stopped. He was sitting in front of the graves and to his right, on a large outcropping of rock, the quartz made a crescent shape. Oli walked to the spot and climbed onto some rocks to see the quartz closer. Taking a step, he heard a rock drop. Looking around, Oli realized that it had fallen inside something, not outside.

Dropping to his knees next to the pile of rocks, Oli started moving them away. Under the rocks he found an opening to a cave. In his excitement, Oli threw the rest of the rocks out of the way. The sun was now hot in the box canyon and the air was stale. Sweat was running down his back.

Oli tossed the deerskin coat to the side and continued to make the opening bigger. Entering the cave, he found that it was about three feet wide and four feet high. Tool marks on the walls told him that it was man-made. He crawled about 10 feet in when his hand felt something move when he bumped it. In the low light, Oli was not sure if it was stone chips or something else. Picking it up he sat back heavily against the wall. It was a gold coin!

"Jolly, it is here, it is here!" Oli shouted. Tears began to flow down his face.

As Oli's eyes adjusted to the low light, he saw a stone shelf. The gold coins and bars were neatly piled on the shelf. He crawled back out of the cave and into the bright light. Crossing over, he sat in front of the three graves. His emotions were going wild. He wanted to shout, cry, and dance. He wanted to thank God for delivering him here. Unable to control himself, he began to shake.

A gust of cold air brought him back to reality. Clouds were rolling in, and the temperature was dropping. He put his deerskin coat back on. Time was running short, and soon snow would be falling. Oli went back to his camp. He now wished that he had the saddlebags, and softly cussed at Jed.

135

He took one of his canvas packs and began to sew it into two bags. He then took the blanket and cut pieces to reinforce the bags. He sewed straps onto them to allow them to hang over the back of the good horse.

The sun was low when Oli returned to the cave. Putting gold into the bags, he struggled to get them outside. He then carefully replaced the stones, closing up the opening. That night, sitting next to his small fire and drinking a brew made from roasted hazelnuts, Oli worked on a stone, chipping away pieces with another smaller stone. It was much like the cavemen would have done.

As the sun came up, Oli was wrapped in his ground tarp, sleeping near his cold campfire. He opened his eyes and blinked as a snow flake hit him square in the eye. Oli sat up quickly. The snow was light and he hoped that it would not amount to much.

Picking up the stone that he had been working on, he set it at the foot of the three graves. Oli had chipped three crosses on the stone. He then knelt and said a quiet prayer over the graves. The men had probably helped mine the gold, and were then killed in a battle, receiving nothing more than isolated graves. Oli felt that he needed to do something to thank them.

He replaced the map inside his coat. Taking out his ledger, he checked his assets.

1 wool shirt, 1 wool pants, 1 pair woolen socks, 1 long underwear, 1 pair boots, 1

darning needle, 1 leather awl, 1 good knife, 1 razor, 1 canteen, 2 fish hooks, 1 deerskin coat, 1 hat, 1 belt, 1 ground tarp, 1 tent, 2 flints, 1 cook pot, 1 mess kit (cup, plate, bowl, spoon), 1 Kentucky long rifle, powder, ball, oil, patches, 1 good horse, bridle and rig, 1 buffalo hide, food for 7 days (dried buffalo meat and plums)

Oli looked at the list. He could be worse off. He had his money belt and the gold. He estimated that the gold weighed 100 pounds. If he could make it back east, he would no longer want for anything.

He thought again about the distance that he had to travel to get home. He thought about the time spent smoking and drying meat to be eaten later. He shook his head, everything took too much time.

Oli placed the gold on the good horse, along with the buffalo hide wrapped around a few things. The cold wind coming off the mountain brought swirling snow. He stopped at the mouth of the box canyon and looked back.

Turning to look east at what lay before him, he rubbed the animal's neck. "Good horse, this is what I brought you along for. I cannot carry my pack and the gold. You do this for me and I will feed you corn and oats for the rest of your days."

With the cold fall wind blowing against their backs, two lonely figures walked east.

CHAPTER TEN

Oli sat on a bank above the Bighorn River. The sun was shining, but the wind blew cold. Every morning the ground was covered with frost. The good horse would nuzzle the ground, looking for anything edible, with clouds of steam rising every time she exhaled.

He looked at the good horse pulling at the sparse grass. Oli wished that he could give the good horse better feed. She was losing weight. The ribs stood out on her sides. Oli knew that he was also losing. His pants were getting looser. He had punched new holes in his belt twice.

Forced to walk every day, they were not getting enough to eat. Oli had found some choke cherries earlier that day. The good horse stood beside him, pulling some off the bushes.

"Eat up good horse, we got to take advantage of any food we find."

Snorting, the animal pushed Oli a bit to get to some more cherries. He understood how good a friend a man's horse was out in the wilds. Yesterday, he had spent quite a bit of time picking hazelnuts. The good horse enjoyed chewing them. Oli ate his share, breaking them on a rock with the handle of his good knife.

He had no idea how long it would take to get home. It had taken months to get from St. Louis to the mountains. Oli realized that he would have to spend the winter somewhere. He had not seen a soul since Jed. He was concerned about his future. This was Cheyenne and Black Foot territory. On occasion, he would open the pack of gold and look at it. He always felt better afterword.

The days were growing shorter. The leaves were gone. Trees stood tall with their naked arms reaching towards the sky. Clumps of evergreens were dark against the hills. Oli continued to walk toward the rising sun, leading the good horse. This morning he had to make new soles out of the buffalo hide for his boots. He'd used a double thickness and hoped that it would last a month.

The good horse tugged at its lead rope. Oli stopped and looked at her foreleg. The tendons were getting larger. He wrapped strips of buffalo hide around them to give more support. The good horse's bones were showing more every day. Oli worried as he ate a small, cold meal. It was leftover fish from breakfast. He had caught two nice trout the night before.

The good horse stood through the midday meal break with its head hanging. Her coat had gotten thicker and rougher looking. Oli decided that he needed to let the good horse rest for a couple days. He made camp next to a nameless stream. He spent time rubbing the good horse down with handfuls of grass. He spent two days looking for any grass or tender shoots to feed her. He warmed water in his cook pot and let the good horse drink.

Mornings would often greet them with a light covering of snow. The sun would melt it off during the day, leaving patches in the shaded areas. Oli and the good horse slowly made their way in an easterly direction. He made sure that they kept to some kind of cover and did not outline themselves on hills.

One evening, Oli was making camp and he saw smoke in the distance. He asked himself, when does one give up, just walk towards the smoke, and accept whatever is at the end? He knew the answer: Never! He made a large circle around the smoke, taking time that he felt they could ill afford. He was cautious about shooting at game, out of fear of being heard. Jed's scenario came to mind. There were just six musket balls left and enough powder to fire them. Oli was using pieces of his shirt for patches.

He boiled some pine nuts in his pot. It gave the water flavor as he washed down smoke dried venison. He had taken a chance and shot a deer a week ago. The meat was going fast. After drinking the hot water, Oli gave the pine nuts to the good horse. It seemed to pick her up a bit.

Wrapped in his coat and the ground tarp, he looked east. He could see low mountains covered with evergreens. He was several days walk from them. Oli draped the tent canvas over the good horse. She was standing three-legged, favoring the front leg. He draped the buffalo hide over himself and lay down, using the gold for a pillow. The hardness of the gold would wake him up every hour with a sore head. It was his way of checking on things through the night.

Oli had been hearing wolves. Each night they were closer. Sleeping fitfully, he looked at the stars and estimated that it was three hours before daylight. He looked over at the good horse. She was lying on her side! Oli went over to check on the good horse. When he rubbed her neck she did not respond.

"No! No!" Oli cried.

He arranged the tent over the good horse and then sat down, cradling her head in his lap. He rubbed the animal's neck. She snorted softly and nibbled at Oli's hand when he rubbed her nose. As the sun came up, the good horse shuddered and stopped breathing.

Oli sat unmoving for an hour, with the good horse's head in his lap. He made promises of how he would bury her and not let wild animals get to her. Tears ran down his cheeks and he continued to talk softly to the departed friend.

He started stacking stones over the good horse. He stood back looking at his work of the last hour, just not enough stones. He had mostly covered the good horse. No doubt animals would dig into the stones. At least they would have to work at it to get to her.

Oli looked at the large stack of packs he would have to carry. He had discarded the pack rig, the tent, and fortunately he didn't have too much food to carry. He estimated that his pack would be about 150 pounds, plus the long rifle.

Lifting the packs onto his back, he felt the straps cut into his shoulders. Stumbling along, he began to walk east. After an hour, he had to stop and rest. He cut and folded pieces of the buffalo hide and put them under the straps on his shoulders. About a half hour later, Oli heard howling and snarling behind him. The cold, clear air carried the sound well.

"They found you already, old friend," Oli whispered.

By midday he was exhausted. He broke one of his own rules and built a bigger fire. He heated water and put the rest of the deer meat in. Slowly, he drank the broth and chewed the pieces of meat. Snow began to fall.

Oli struggled for two days. The snow was a foot deep. His toes were numb. He stomped his feet to try and improve circulation. Every time he breathed, the hair in his nose would freeze. His scruffy blond beard protected his face from frost bite. He had to rest often to prevent sweating. He would surely freeze during the night if this happened.

The low, dark mountains were getting larger. He did not dare shoot at game. The noise would attract notice, and he just didn't have enough extra balls to waste one on a small animal.

While he sat taking one of many rests, Oli heard a scraping noise. He saw a porcupine climbing a balsam tree. He moved below the tree. Reaching for his knife, he let it fly and was on target. The porcupine kicked at the air and became still. It was caught in the branches. In frustration, he shook the tree vigorously. The porcupine broke loose and fell, glancing off his shoulder. Oli felt a stinging on his cheek from the quills.

Pulling his knife out of the animal, Oli wiped the blood off in the snow. Then, picking it up by the leg, he carried it over to his packs. Looking at his shoulder, Oli saw several quills stuck in the deerskin coat. He touched his cheek, looking for quills intermingled in his beard. Thanks to the cold weather, he didn't feel too much pain as he removed them.

With all the quills removed from the coat and cheek, he went to work skinning the porcupine. The roasted animal tasted wonderful. It was just over an hour from dark, so he decided to spend the night.

Shaking the snow off some shorter balsams, he draped his ground tarp over the top of them. He removed some of the inside branches to create a hole, then put the buffalo skin down to sleep on. He could fold half of it over as a cover. He built the fire up to warm the small shelter. He melted snow and heated water. Oli drank it to warm his insides. Looking past the fire, he saw something move.

Wolves! Swearing to himself, he had no intention of becoming their next meal. Using his gold pillow trick, Oli kept the fire going through the night. He walked a few steps to the side of his shelter to relieve himself.

He could see wolf tracks around the perimeter, and could see where they had sat and watched him sleep. Right now, the smell of man disturbed them and they kept their distance. He knew as days wore on the fear would disappear.

Oli picked up the leftover porcupine. It was frozen solid. He combined snow and the porcupine meat in the pot and warmed it by the fire. He had a less than satisfying breakfast. He packed everything and swung it onto his back and moved out, always heading east.

He trudged on ahead of the wolves, with panic slowly rising. Looking back, he could see three wolves. He was sure that there were more. The Kentucky long rifle was charged and ready.

The sun was going down, and Oli stopped to make camp in a grove of spruce. He pulled some branches in and then laced more in to give some protection from the elements. Cutting blocks of snow with the good knife, he stacked them to make a wind break. He started a fire in front of the opening.

By tomorrow, he would be near the small mountains. Nothing would change in his world, but he needed a goal to keep going. He started a fire and then walked to the stream to get water. It was covered with three inches of ice. Using a rock to break a hole, it took several tries before the ice gave way. He carried the pot of water back to his fire. He attempted to take a drink from the pot and his lip and tongue stuck to the metal edge.

A large male wolf sat 40 feet away, staring at his future meal, his black and pink tongue hanging out. Well, Oli decided, two can play the game. He also needed a meal. Drawing a bead on the chest of the wolf, he squeezed off a shot. The rifle was loud in the shelter. The wolf yelped and flipped in a complete circle and fell dead. Oli knew they ate their own, so he rushed out and got the dead wolf and dragged it to the shelter. It was easily over 100 pounds.

Sitting by the fire, he skinned the wolf and dropped pieces of meat in the steaming pot of water. He took the liver and stuck it on a stick, roasting it over the fire. Oli chewed on the liver while he watched the pot boil. It was not the best liver he had eaten, but he was really hungry. The eyes of the other wolves glowed in the darkness. He dipped strips of meat from the pot. The meat was fatty. The wolves had been eating well. The wolf meat tasted quite good.

Oli jumped when he heard something behind his shelter. The wolves were circling him. They were closer than last night. He laced more branches into the sides and back of his shelter. He built up the fire in front.

Sitting, staring at the glowing eyes, he realized that he was not going to win. He no longer got pleasure looking at the gold. It had become a yoke around his neck. The snow began falling, with the flakes sizzling on the fire.

To keep his mind off his situation, Oli began to scrape the wolf hide. It would work well as a foot warmer. To keep awake, he cooked all the meat, cooling and freezing it on the snow. He had five shots left for the long rifle, barring a misfire. Oli knew that he had not been able to clean the weapon in weeks.

Oli made one of his toughest decisions. He would have to stash the gold somewhere and then go and find shelter. He could return later to get the gold. He would walk one more day with both packs. The good meal of wolf meat should make that possible.

He woke to his first blizzard. The wind was howling and everything was white. He was thankful that he had made the wind break. The blowing snow went over the break, with some drifting onto his side.

Oli crawled around, searching for wood. He was sure that the wolves were having just as much trouble as he was keeping warm, and would not be hunting. His hand felt a four inch-thick windfall next to his shelter. Pulling it in close, he cut the branches off as he fed the trunk into his fire.

Once, crawling out to go relieve himself, Oli became confused and could not remember which way was back to the shelter. With his heart pounding, he slowly moved along, groping to find the shelter. He bumped against a large drift. He decided to burrow into the drift for protection from the wind. Moving around to the other side of the drift to dig, he found himself in front of the shelter.

Shaking more from almost getting lost in the storm than from the cold, he built the fire up a bit more. Sometime during the night the storm stopped. Oli knew that he had to move on. He ate some of the wolf meat and drank warm water. He had a few meals of meat left. For the moment, the wolves were gone.

CHAPTER ELEVEN

Oli left the shelter an hour after sun up. Light snow was still falling. It was getting close to two feet deep. He hoped that the wind would not come up again. He just was not ready for that. The extra weight of the wolf meat and skin were noticeable. When he found an area that was blown clear, Oli was thankful that it was easier to walk.

The wind was starting to pick up, and he could feel the snow stinging his face. He tried walking backwards to give his face a break from the wind and snow. It was not practical. His fingers were stiff inside the buffalo skin mittens. His feet felt like he was walking on two clubs.

Behind him, Oli heard the wolves make short work of the remains of the large male. He knew that they would follow his nicely-packed trail. He did not dare to stop. Sweat was forming on his skin. Pushing through the snow blindly, Oli knew that his time was short. He would never be able to build a shelter and get warm tonight. The wolves were too close.

Looking back, he saw them moving through the trees on his back trail. Oli swung around and aimed at the lead wolf. They had gotten smarter. The wolf leaped out of the track and disappeared into the trees.

Oli found the windblown snow more difficult to walk through. The crust would not hold his weight, and breaking trail was hard work. He tripped over a windfall under the snow. Sprawling ahead, his heavy packs almost knocked the wind out of him. He struggled to his feet just in time.

He pointed the now useless rifle toward the wolves trotting towards him and they once again jumped off the trail and into the woods. He noticed that they could run on top of the drifted snow.

When getting up, Oli had to wiggle out of his packs. There was snow down his neck. He had lost one of the gloves when trying to get up. With stiff fingers, he dug the snow out from under his collar. His hand grew numb before he could find his mitten and put it back on.

He made up his mind. He would walk as long as he could. Then, before the wolves got to him, he would open the arteries in his neck. Oli didn't want to feel the hot breath and teeth on his body.

Taking hold of the packs, he lifted them. He stopped in mid-lift. When he fell he had knocked the snow off a low stump. The stump showed evidence of an axe! With his eyes watering from the blowing snow, Oli looked slowly around him. He saw what looked like a roof line through the trees.

Walking ahead, dragging the packs and using the long rifle as a walking stick, he went toward what might be a cabin. As he got closer, he saw horizontal logs. Letting go of the bags of gold, Oli clung to the supply pack and long rifle. He stumbled ahead. He found a door with the latchstring out. Pulling on the string, it broke off. Taking his knife with numb hands, he worked it in the crack of the door and lifted the bar. Pushing hard, he fell ahead. As he fell he felt something hit him in the back. Oli rolled in the middle of the cabin. Turning, he yelled and waved his arms at the wolf that stood in the doorway. The strong smell of man was too much for the animal, and it ran off a ways and sat down.

Oli could see little in the dim interior. He had to leave the door open for light. Feeling around, his hand came down on a candle.

"This will work well once I get a fire started," Oli chuckled. He was feeling exhilarated. He was not going to die today.

Continuing to search around, Oli could make out the fireplace. Feeling around in it, he felt lots of ash. Someone had lit a fire, then went away and let it go out. Groping around the edge of the fireplace, he found tinder and kindling.

Pushing the ash back out of the way, he built a mound of tinder. He fumbled to get a piece of flint from his pocket. He had a difficult time holding the knife and flint with his numb hands. Oli began to shiver from the sweat on his skin. His first try, he dropped the flint. It was difficult to locate with numb fingers. After several failed attempts, he finally got the fire started. As the fire licked up around the wood, he stretched his numb hands to the flames. His hands felt like a thousand needles poking when the heat reached them.

His eyes began to burn and he coughed from the smoke. The chimney was plugged. Coughing, Oli stumbled towards the light in the doorway. Sticking his head out, he checked to see if the wolves were close. He need not have worried. Smoke was pouring out the door and the wolves had moved even further back.

Oli went around the cabin and climbed on the low back eave. A branch had fallen over the top of the chimney and falling snow had closed it off. With his teeth chattering, he carefully cleared off the snow, and removed the branch.

Smoke billowed out into the crisp air. Oli held his hands over the top of the chimney for a moment, enjoying the warm smoke. Sliding off the roof, he went back into the cabin. The smoke still stung his eyes. Looking around, he saw the pile of wood. He put more onto the fire and soon the fireplace was blazing.

Lighting the candle, he moved around the cabin. Oli froze in his tracks. On the bed lay the skeletal remains of the owner. His right leg and foot lay on the floor. The leg bone appeared to be broken.

There was a note lying on the bed next to the deceased. Moving over to shut the door, Oli walked back to the fireplace. As the warmth of the fire reached him, he felt his legs weakening. The adrenalin of finding safety was gone and fatigue overtook him.

He decided to take care of the dead man in the morning. Sitting next to the fireplace, Oli took some wolf meat from the pack he had dragged in. Warming it a bit on the fireplace, he ate it down. Then, curling up on the floor, he went to sleep.

He slept dreamless, exhausted sleep. He woke several hours later, feeling the chill in the room. The fireplace had self-banked, so getting another fire started was quick. Feeling somewhat rested, he began to look more closely around the cabin.

Oli saw some cans on a shelf near a small table. He found coffee in one of the cans. Filling the coffee pot he'd found with snow, soon there was boiling water. He carefully measured grounds into the pot. There was a cup on the table. Blowing the dust out of it, Oli enjoyed the first cup of coffee in weeks. Going over to the bed, he got the note.

To whoever finds this,

My name is Don Sikes. I have been laid up here now for two weeks. The leg is looking bad. It is the winter of 37. I need to cut the leg off. Broke it when I stepped through the ice. If I survive, I will make the morning fire with this paper. If not, you are welcome to my stuff. If you ever get to Philadelphia let them know what happened to me.

Don Sikes

Oli sat looking at the letter for the longest time. He suddenly felt ashamed of thinking of ending his life yesterday. Here was a man who fought for life right to the end. It was a lesson to learn. He walked over to the bed and looked down at the brave, unfortunate man.

It was too cold to bury Don Sikes. Oli carefully placed the leg back onto the bed and wrapped Don Sikes in the buffalo robe cover he had died on. Clearing a space, he gentle placed him in the corner of the cabin. The late Mr. Sikes weighed very little.

He didn't want to leave him outside, where the wolves could gnaw and scatter his bones. Besides, it would be good to have the company of a brave man for the winter.

Oli looked the cabin over from end to end. If things were not in tins, rodents or small animals had dragged them away. Even the powder horn was chewed in half and the powder scattered. Don had lead and a mold for making more musket balls. The caliber was right for the long rifle. Don's rifle was leaning in a corner that had a leak. It was rusted beyond repair.

Oli found some oil and using it and hot water, he cleaned the long rifle. Having it loaded again, he walked to the door. Opening it, he saw three wolves setting near a line of trees. Drawing a bead on the largest, he fired. The wolf yipped and jumped to the side. A few kicks later, it lay still. Oli hurried to the wolf and dragged it back to the cabin.

As he closed the door, he saw the other wolves fighting over the bloody snow. He shuddered and prepared to skin the animal. Sitting at the table, Oli watched the leg of wolf roast in the fireplace. Was he wrong to eat the wolves? They would have eaten him, he thought.

Looking around, there was a rusty tin lying next to the opposite wall. He found it to be filled with salt. The salt was now a solid block, but nothing could have looked better. Food with taste! Scraping a little off the block, Oli rubbed it onto the wolf leg.

For the next couple days, he cleaned the cabin from end to end. With the cabin warmed up, leaks in the roof appeared. Oli's solution was to keep things away from the dripping areas. The floor was hard-packed dirt. A single window originally had oil paper covering it. Now it was shuttered. There was a large pile of wood on the side of the cabin.

The cabin was small, and when the fireplace was going well he was able to keep the door ajar for extra light. An exciting find was a cap and ball gun under the bed. Don may have had it there in case the suffering became too bad. No, Oli decided. It did not fit his image of the brave Mr. Sikes. In his search, he found enough cap and balls to load the revolver two more times.

Oli covered the bed with his buffalo hide and a rodent-chewed blanket he had found. As he went to bed, he turned to Don lying in the corner.

"I thank, you my friend, for your hospitality. Your people will know what happened to you." The leather straps on the bed creaked as he lay down. Soon, he was fast asleep.

The wind was howling when Oli awoke. The area was in the middle of a full-blown blizzard. The wind swirled down the chimney and would blow sparks on the floor. Snow filtered in through cracks in the logs where the chinking had fallen out. The barred door rattled to the point where he expected it to fly off the leather hinges.

Donning the deerskin coat, Oli stepped out into the storm. He clung to the wall as he made his way to the wood pile. He had to work by feel. The blowing snow blinded him. When he stepped around the corner, the wind knocked him back. He was impressed. This had to be the king of storms.

The wind howled for five days. The morning after the storm, the quiet was as alarming as the wind had been. Oli opened the door. The snow was chest high in front of the cabin. He looked out at a transformed world. Everything was pure white. He saw drifts as high as two men.

Pushing his way out of the door, Oli glanced in the direction he had come from. Somewhere out there was the gold. He had not forgotten about it. He figured that it would stay where he'd dropped it until he had a chance to go look for it. Burrowing through the snow, he got a large arm load of wood.

Sitting next to the fire, Oli knew that he had to get out and hunt. Don had traps in the cabin. Oli could set these and maybe catch something to eat. He found a pair of snow shoes hanging on wall near the fireplace, then strapped them to his feet. He tucked the revolver into his belt and picked up the long rifle.

Ready, he went out to hunt. The snow was drifted, and firm. The snowshoes creaked as he walked. The air was cold and he kept his neckerchief over his face. By mid-morning he found a deer yard a mile away from the cabin. Oli shot a large doe.

While dragging it back, he harvested another wolf that thought it could take the deer from him. Oli smiled as he tucked the handgun back in his belt. Once in the cabin, he skinned and butchered the two animals. This meat would take him through six weeks.

He looked through the rest of Don Sikes' supplies. One tin had corn meal. Yet another had molasses. Oli started making mush with molasses for breakfast. Enjoying the hot mush, he felt like it was a holiday meal.

Looking over at Don Sikes, he asked, "Do you want to sing some Christmas carols with me?" Oli sang every song he could remember. He and the departed Mr. Sikes were in good voice.

Oli went outside after a three-day blow in February and was surprised to find the front of the cabin blown clear of snow. The bags of gold were lying in plain sight in a crust of ice. He broke them loose and brought them into the cabin.

They were looking good again. He dug a hole under the bed and hid the gold, then tamped the dirt back down to hide the location. All things considered, Oli had had a pretty good winter, thanks to Don. The wolves finally got the message and moved out of the area.

There was a winter thaw in late February. Oli sat outside with his coat off, patching his socks, enjoying the fresh breeze. March was just a cold, snowy month. The wind seemed to howl every day. Biting snow made moving around outdoors miserable.

Oli had let his beard grow all winter for the protection. He found himself talking to Don by the hour. When the wood ran out, Oli took the bucksaw from near the depleted wood pile and went out to cut additional wood.

On the morning when he woke up hearing water dripping both outside and inside, he leaped from his bed and stepped out to the first spring day.

* * *

Oli had not changed his mind about stashing the gold. He realized that it was just too much weight for one man to carry out. With the snow gone, he found a perfect place to hide the gold. Across the valley from the small mountain, there was a naturally formed cave in a rock ledge. It had a large oak tree next to it, larger than any other tree in the area. It would be easy to locate when he came back.

The cave was dry and ran back about 15 feet. Oli placed all but 10 pounds of the gold inside the cave. Taking his time, he stacked rocks part way into the cave and against the opening until it was securely closed. He then covered it again with a more random arrangement of stones. Stepping back, it looked quite natural. Looking across the valley, he could see the cabin.

He walked back to the cabin and turned to Don. "My good friend, it is time to go to your final resting place."

Oli found a shovel and dug a nice, deep hole for Don. The grave was lined up with the cave. Laying Don Sikes to rest, he filled the hole and put a mound of stones on top. Looking around the grave, he saw blue flowers growing everywhere. He carefully dug several and planted them at the foot of Don's grave. Oli then spent a week chipping out a headstone for Don.

Don Sikes
1837
A Friend

He placed the stone facing squarely toward the cave. "That should do it," he smiled.

Oli said a short prayer over Don. He stood by the grave for quite some time, looking around the flower-covered valley. Spring was breaking out everywhere. He dearly wished that the good horse was here to enjoy the fresh green grass.

He sat at the table with his ledger and made a list of his assets.

1 wool shirt, 1 wool pants, 1 pair woolen socks, 1 long underwear, 1 pair boots, 1 darning, needle, 1 leather awl, 1 good knife, 1 razor, 1 deerskin coat, 1 hat, 1 belt, 1 ground tarp, 1 flint, 1 canteen, 1 cook pot, 1 coffee pot, 1 Kentucky long rifle, powder, ball, oil, patches, 1 fishing line and hook, 1 buffalo hide, 1 wolf skin, 1 deer skin, 1 cap and ball gun, 1 short handle axe, 1 mess kit (cup, plate, bowl, spoon), food for 14 days (deer jerky, salt, coffee)

Before heading out, Oli replaced the soles of his boots again. He double checked the sketch of the valley in his ledger and then he put the pack together and hefted it.

Stepping back, he nodded. "About 110 pounds. That's a nice size pack."

The weather was cool, so Oli wore his deerskin coat. The money belt was stuffed with gold coins. He carried the ledger in his coat pocket, the revolver in his waist, and the long rifle cradled in his arm. He walked east, feeling truly free. He was traveling light and fast.

He worked his way up the Cheyenne River, towards the Missouri River. The north side of the river had good animal trails, so Oli chose this side to travel. The second day, along the Cheyenne River, he saw an Indian village. He walked away from the river, heading cross country towards the Missouri. He still couldn't get the vision of Jed out of his head.

CHAPTER TWELVE

Two weeks later, Oli arrived at the Missouri River, well north of where the Cheyenne River would meet it. He didn't have any idea how far he was from the Mississippi River and St. Louis. He knew that if he stayed on the river he would find civilization. While in St. Louis, he could prepare for the trip back to get the gold.

Oli took his short-handled axe and cut enough trees to build a raft. He cut the deerskin into strips to secure the logs together. Braiding a line 14 feet long, he used it to tie the raft up. The water was high, due to spring floods. He pondered that. Every time he was on the river the water was high.

He had caught four nice catfish. So he had an excellent breakfast before shoving off. Floating down the river was very relaxing. Oli had a push pole to keep the raft away from snags. He enjoyed the new foliage on the banks of the river. Geese flew by in great flocks, heading north to their nesting areas.

Wood ducks flew by, rapidly changing direction as they went.

The day was warm and Oli was dozing on the raft. He heard a zip in the water beside the raft, followed shortly by a *tunk* on the back of the raft. He looked up just in time to see two canoes closing in on him.

One of the Cheyenne let an arrow fly. Oli threw himself flat onto the raft as the arrow narrowly missed him. Pulling the cap and ball gun out of his waistband, he fired at the canoe. The ball tore through the birch bark side and hit one of the Indians' legs. He fired at the other canoe. The ball shattered the paddle and tore an ugly gash in the Indian's arm. The canoes slowed down.

Taking the long rifle out, Oli watched the Indians debate whether they should continue to attack or go back. With little to gain on the raft, they decided to abandon the chase. Oli continued to float on throughout the day and the next night. The moon was full, and he was anxious to put distance between the Cheyenne and himself. At least he was pretty sure that they were Cheyenne.

He pulled over a couple hours before daylight and tied up to a snag sticking out of the river. Exhausted, Oli wrapped up in the deerskin coat and was quickly asleep. The river flowing by gently rocked the raft, bumping it against the snag.

Oli did not notice as the raft broke loose. Slowly turning, the raft floated downriver. They started to go faster as the raft entered the rapids. It bounced off a rock, waking Oli. Confused, he tried to figure what was happening. He heard a roaring of the water ahead. A waterfall?

Panic struck him, and he grabbed out for a log sticking out from the river bank. Clinging to the log, he watched the raft and his stuff careen down the steep rapids. The raft bounced from rock to rock, breaking into pieces.

He slowly moved along the log and up on the bank. Wet to the waist, he was thankful to be on dry land. Seeing a path used by animals traveling along the river, Oli jumped up and ran down to see if he could salvage any of his belongings. With brush on each side of the path, it was more like a tunnel.

Oli stopped at the crest of the falls and looked over the boulders. Quickly, he ducked back down after he spotted a canoe with two braves. Looking carefully around the side of the boulder, he saw that they were picking up whatever was floating. The Indians were shouting to some canoes downriver.

He figured they might be looking for the owner of the items. Running back upriver a way, Oli turned up a stream flowing into the river. He walked in the middle to prevent any tracks. He continued to blindly go up the stream, the brush slapping his face, until late afternoon.

Tired and lost, Oli sat on the bank, looking back the way he had come. He pulled his deerskin coat around his shoulders and pondered his fate.

"What did I do wrong to have this bad luck? Was it because I abandoned my goals and chased riches instead?"

Looking up to the heavens, he asked, "Lord, what did I do to deserve this?"

With much effort and little enthusiasm, Oli walked upstream until he found a bend that was surrounded by low trees. It created a small, grassy peninsula. The money belt was heavy and cutting into his back. Oli's legs ached, and his feet were burning from the chafing caused by the water in his shoes.

He sank down onto the grass. He touched his bruised face, looking for any cuts, remembering the brush on the stream banks. Exhaustion overcame him and he curled up in the grass and slept. The sun was low in the sky when he awoke. He was sore and hungry. Remembering his father's advice, he knew that it was time to check his assets. It was the only way he could make the next several decisions.

Slipping the ledger from the deerskin coat pocket, he opened it up. Taking the pencil stub, he wet the end.

1 wool shirt, 1 wool pants, 1 pair woolen socks, 1 long underwear, 1 pair boots, 1 belt, 1 darning needle, 1 good knife, 1 deerskin coat, 1 hat, 1 neckerchief

Oli was now working with a short list. The darning needle was kept in the crease of the ledger. That was the only reason he still had it. He had the money belt stuffed with gold. It was hard to eat gold, though.

He figured that it was May 1840. He was hungry and tired. He looked around and saw wild onions. Picking them, he sat chewing and thinking. If he went back to the river and continued down, he would be taking the chance of meeting hostiles.

He wouldn't have to go too far east before he would be through the plains and into wooded areas. His biggest problem would be fire. His flint had gone with the raft. With his knife he could make a bow and cut some arrows. He could get some smaller game. He would have to eat it raw. While it was unappetizing right now, Oli knew that as he got hungrier the distaste would disappear.

Oli had seen people start fire rubbing sticks and wood. He did not hold out too much hope of being able to do this. Standing in the waning sun, He figured that it was time to start working with what he had left. While he should continue east, he decided to rest and prepare for a few days, to improve chances of survival.

* * *

Oli selected a straight sapling about an inch and a half thick and seven feet long. Cutting the sapling down, he removed the bark and carefully sharpened a point on one end. He now had an acceptable spear and walking stick.

Then, carefully cutting strips from the bottom of his deerskin coat, Oli pulled several saplings together and tied them, creating a dome. He weaved reeds in among the saplings, creating an acceptable roof. He then dragged windfalls to each side of the shelter, creating a lower wall.

Oli found a one foot-thick and four feet-long section of log, chewed off on each end by beavers. He dragged, rolled, tipped and pushed it to the front of his shelter. It would be a comfortable seat during the day. Stepping back as dusk set in, he admired his brush hut.

He laughed, "Not a beautiful home, but it has a woodsy charm."

Oli covered the floor with last fall's leaves. Now it was fully dark. He climbed into the shelter and curled up on the leaves. While he knew that he was not much better off than when he walked into this area, it gave him a good feeling to know he had improved on his condition.

He emerged from his shelter with the morning sun high in the sky. Sitting on the log with his spear in his hand, Oli worried a little about sleeping so soundly. Moving to the stream for a drink of water, he noticed some crayfish swimming along the bottom. He caught a half-dozen and sat back on the bank and ate them. They tasted a lot like mud. He ate them, shell and all, which made them chewy and crunchy. He found some more onions and ate them to get the mud taste out of his mouth.

Today, Oli figured, he would make a bow. Taking a four foot sapling, he tapered and notched the ends. He then chose several small, straight branches. One end he sharpened and on the other he put a notch.

Oli cut a narrow groove into the notched end. He fitted a shaved piece of wood into this groove. Unraveling some wool from his shirt sleeve, he lashed the shaved wood to the arrow. This would act to keep the arrow flying straight. He could only put it on one side. If he put one on the bow side, it would be knocked off when firing.

With six acceptable arrows, Oli again cut a strip from the bottom of his coat for a bow string. He knew that the leather would stretch. He planned to only string the bow when he had something to shoot at.

He took a test shot. He was wide of the target, but it worked! He continued to make things that would make life easier. A reed door shut the world out at night. A wooden stand gave him someplace to keep things off the ground.

Oli left the grove he called home and walked quietly with the bow. He spent four hours before he managed to bag a prairie chicken. Walking back into his camp, Oli looked forward to something other than crayfish to eat.

Knowing that he could not afford to waste anything, Oli plucked the feathers and saved them in the corner of his shelter. As he cut the bird up, he licked the blood that appeared. He ate the liver first. It was tender and easy to chew.

When he was young he had read about the Tartars, who were nomads in Asia. They would put their meat under their horses' saddles and ride on it for the day to tenderize it. Oli decide that he could do something similar to his meat. To make the bird's flesh easier to eat, he deboned it and pounded the meat between two stones.

The result was acceptable. Oli did not kid himself. He was not getting enough food. New holes in his belt were a record of a man starving.

One evening, just before dark, a raccoon ambled by, looking for crayfish in the stream. Without thinking, Oli drew and threw the knife. It sunk to the hilt in the side of the raccoon. Chattering, it ran off into the brush.

Oli shouted, "My knife! My knife!" and he ran blindly through the brush after the raccoon.

A half hour later, he returned without the raccoon or knife. He spent a sleepless night. At first light, he went back to the point where he'd thrown the knife. Starting from the stream, he found a blood trail leading into the brush. Slowly, he tracked the raccoon. He lost the trail and backtracked until he found it again.

Moving back and forth, he continued in the direction the raccoon had gone in. He almost missed the tail sticking out from under a gnarled root structure of an oak. The raccoon had tried to push under the roots when it was dying.

Oli worked the stiff carcass of the raccoon out from the roots. Relief swept over him as he saw the hilt of the knife. He was skinning the raccoon when he got a whiff of wood smoke.

Setting the raccoon aside, he went back to the oak tree, climbed up into the branches, and looked up and down the stream. He stayed there for about two hours until he was sure that no threat was around.

Back in his camp, Oli finished deboning the raccoon. Picking up his pounding stone, he had second thoughts. Pounding the meat might be too noisy. Instead, he slid the meat between the stones. It was somewhat mushy as he chewed it for supper.

Oli had a hard time falling asleep that night. He kept hearing noises beyond his camp. He tried to convince himself that these were the same noises he had heard every night. When Oli would start to doze, he would see the faces of warriors coming at him in full war paint. He would sit up, startled and sweating despite the cool evening.

When morning came, Oli crawled out of his shelter and sat on the log, drifting in and out of sleep. He was dreaming of sitting near a fire and adding wood to it. He awoke as he almost slipped off the log.

Shaking his head, Oli stopped. He could still smell the smoke of the fire. It was not a dream. Something was burning. Getting his bearings from the wind direction, he determined that it was coming from the west.

A plan formulated in his mind. If he could locate the source of the fire, he could wait until the fire maker left. With luck, there would be coals left and he could get some for his own fire.

Picking up the raccoon skin, Oli loaded the rest of the meat into it. Securing it to his belt, he worked his way quietly west along the stream. About a quarter-mile along, the smoke became stronger.

He located a small grove of cottonwood a short distance away. From what he could determine, this would be the best location for the fire. Oli pulled the good knife from its sheath. Crawling forward, careful not to break twigs, or brush up against branches, he inched ahead. Half of the remaining distance took him an hour.

Lying and watching, Oli could see smoke from a dying fire curling up into the morning air. He had moved as far as he dared toward the fire. Any closer and he would be exposed. He continued to watch the fire as the smoke disappeared. He knew that he could not wait too much longer.

All of a sudden, he caught some movement ahead. It was low to the ground and he was sure that it was accompanied by a groan. Was an enemy lying in wait for him to become careless? Oli then caught sight of movement to his left. The dark form moved with great stealth towards whatever was near the dying fire.

It was a cat, a cougar maybe. It was stalking something near the fire. Now that the smoke had stopped, it was bravely moving in. Suddenly, the cat leaped forward, after something out of Oli's line of sight. He heard a scream, a woman's scream!

Caution thrown aside, Oli ran toward the camp, shouting and waving his knife. What he found was the last thing he had expected.

The cat was crouched, snarling at Oli after attacking an Indian woman lying huddled on the ground. She had a bloody claw mark on her leg from the cat's initial attack. Grabbing up a stick from near the fire, Oli ran at the cat, waving the stick in one hand and the knife in the other, trying his best to look as big as he could.

Evidently, the cat was less hungry than cautious, and it disappeared into the brush. He looked back and saw the Indian woman trying to crawl into the brush the other way. Oli stepped over to her and knelt.

He could see the terror in her eyes. He was not sure if she was more afraid of him or the cat. Her brown eyes were framed by high cheekbones. She stared unblinking at him. Oli sat back and talked softly to her. She lay curled in a ball near the edge of the brush.

Oli moved over to the fire and added fuel, coaxing the coals back into flames. Watching the woman, he removed some of the raccoon meat from the skin. Skewering it on a branch, Oli broiled the meat. The smell of the cooking meat was heavenly.

He noticed that the woman had moved a bit closer. He handed the cooked meat to her. She was afraid to take it, so he leaned the skewered meat against a log near her. Moving back to the fire, Oli broiled more meat.

Oli sat near the fire chewing the hot, brown meat. Watching her over his meal, she slowly picked up the meat and started eating. Looking around her camp, Oli noticed that she had rigged a sleeping shelter, but no other improvements had been done.

That is, except the fire, which Oli decided was no small feat. Broiling the rest of the raccoon meat, Oli shared it with the woman.

He began to notice some other things that he hadn't seen at first. Her feet were lacerated and covered with crusted blood. She wore a dirty deerskin dress. Her legs, arms, and face were scratched and bruised. Her black hair was disheveled and laced with twigs and grass. What concerned him the most was that she was terribly thin.

After eating the small meal, she curled back up on the ground. Oli nudged her with the stick. There was no response. Building the fire up a little more, he looked around the camp. There was nothing of value that needed moving.

Oli picked up the woman in his arms. He was concerned at how light she was. Carrying her back to his camp, he lay her down in his shelter. He then assembled tinder and wood for his future fire.

Hurrying back to her camp, he looked around for a way to transport the fire. Oli finally decided that a torch would work. Getting the stick that he used to chase the cat, Oli got the end glowing with coals. He then wrapped dry reeds around the end. The reeds began to smolder. Running back to his camp, he thrust the stick, which had just burst into flames, into the tinder.

He fed more wood into the fire. Then he moved stones around the fire. He had not seen any movement from the shelter. Sitting on his log, Oli realized that while he now had fire, getting enough food for two would be a problem. He was barely keeping himself alive, much less another person.

Oli walked up the stream, locating a split rock that he had noticed days before. It had a dip in one surface that would hold about one cup of water. Returning with the 12 pound rock, he placed it next to the fire and, scooping water with his hands, he filled the dip.

He then busied himself improving his spear and arrows. He tempered the points over the fire and then sharpened them. Finishing this task, Oli noticed that the water was hot.

He cut the legs off his long underwear at the knee. Cutting an eight-inch piece from one of the legs, he dipped it into the hot water. Oli moved back and forth between the fire and the woman.

Taking care, he bathed the wounds. On the deeper claw cuts he smeared some pine pitch and then covered them with spider webs. Oli could not remember who had told him this was helpful, but it was all he had to work with, and he hoped that it would help.

Oli remained concerned. All the while he cleaned her legs and feet, she did not move or respond. He knew that it might be too late. While he was refilling the dip in the rock, he heard some geese fly over. They noisily landed nearby.

Grabbing the bow, three arrows, and the spear, Oli crossed the stream and walked up the bank. Crawling to the top, he saw dozens of slender necks and heads looking in his direction.

Sliding down the hill, Oli worked his way along the stream and climbed back up with some brush for cover. Looking through the brush, he could see several dozen geese. Most were busy eating new grass, with the rest keeping watch for any intruders.

Oli could see an area to his right where he could cut the distance between the geese and himself to less than 20 paces without being seen. Quietly crawling over, he looked at the geese. Taking a deep breath, he stood up with a readied bow and let an arrow fly at the closest goose.

He then ran into the midst of the panicked flock, swinging his spear like a club. He felt solid contact with something, and then the geese were gone, flying noisily over the prairie. Looking around, Oli saw a dead goose with an arrow through the vital organs. Another was running, looking for cover, dragging a broken wing.

Oli chased down the wounded goose and leaped on it. The goose turned and bit fiercely at his face.

Its wings beat against his legs. Grabbing the bird's head, Oli ran his knife across the struggling bird's neck.

With the bow slung across his shoulder, Oli walked back toward the camp carrying the two geese. He was lightheaded and his stomach ached with hunger. The spear slipped from under his arm. Glancing back at it, Oli continued toward camp. He could come back after the spear once he had eaten. One of his shoes wobbled loosely on his foot. Looking down, he saw that most of the sole was torn loose.

Arriving at the camp, Oli could see that the Indian woman had not moved. He did notice that her eyes were open and watching him. He started to pluck the goose he had shot. The process was too slow.

He tore the skin off the goose and gutted it. Taking the gizzard and liver, he ran a stick through them and put them over the fire, which was down to coals. He ate them, chewing slowly to get all the benefit of the juices. Sitting for a moment, waiting for the hunger to subside a bit, Oli stared into the woman's eyes. Unblinking, she stared back.

Gathering some more wood for the fire, Oli stoked up the coals and then turned back to cleaning the birds. With one bird roasting over the fire, he gutted the second one. Once again he broiled the gizzard and liver. He brought these to the woman.

"Wa Wa," the woman said. Pointing at the geese she repeated, "Wa Wa."

As she chewed on the meat, Oli made a cup from a water plant leaf and brought it to her. Drinking and chewing, she slowly sat up.

Looking over at her, Oli said, "I guess you have decided that I am not a danger to you."

The aroma of the roasting goose was wonderful. Oli had taken wild onions and put some in the cavity and rubbed the outside with a few more. He knew that without the skin the meat would be dry. He figured that there was lots of water to help with that.

Turning to the Indian woman, Oli tapped on his chest and repeated his name, "Oli August. Oli August."

The woman looked at him and repeated, "Auugus, Auugus."

She then tapped her chest and said, "Huhawira-Nina, Huhawira-Nina."

Smiling, Oli said, "Auugus is close enough, and I will call you Nina."

He pointed to himself. "Auugus." Then to her, "Nina."

She nodded in agreement. Oli finished roasting the first bird and then brought a portion to Nina on a piece of bark. She shrunk back as he approached.

Setting the meat down near her, Oli smiled. "Don't quite trust me yet, huh, Nina?" Sitting alone on his log, Oli quietly ate the very satisfying goose.

With the meal finished Oli brought more water to Nina and then hung the second goose on a limb to keep it away from animals. He dipped the cleansing cloth in some heated water. He moved toward Nina to wash her wounds and lacerations.

She crawled to the back of the shelter, her eyes wide with fright. He made a motion of washing her leg. She pulled back and said something that he was sure meant "No!" Once again, he put the cloth on a piece of bark and laid it inside the shelter.

Walking back to the fire, Oli muttered, "What will she do when I crawl in to go to sleep? I am sure as heck not sleeping outside."

Finishing up the few chores and building up the fire, Oli watched the sun slide down beyond the plain. He was not hungry, he had fire, and he was not alone. This had been a good day.

Oli shook out the deerskin coat and walked to the shelter. He made the gesture of sleeping and began to crawl into the opening. Nina scampered out of the shelter and stopped near the edge of the water.

Shaking his head, Oli settled into the shelter with the coat over him. He fell asleep quickly with the first full stomach he'd had in some time. He could smell the sweat and feel the stiffness of his clothes. He had dried goose blood on his arms. Maybe he should have bathed before crawling into the shelter. He would do that tomorrow.

Oli woke as the sun was coming up. He glanced over. Nina was in the shelter, sleeping as close to the edge as possible. As he got up, Nina jumped and pushed even closer to the side and then froze, looking at him. He crawled out and got the fire going. Then he went to the stream and washed his face and arms.

Getting the goose down from the tree, Oli started plucking it. He was impressed with the amount of feathers the bird had on it. Looking at Nina over his work, Oli noticed that she had cleaned her wounds and had gotten most of the dirt cleaned off her dress and out of her hair. The cat claw cuts looked much better, no doubt the pine pitch and spider webs had worked.

Laying the cleaned bird onto the log, Oli moved over to the stream to wash his hands again. He saw his reflection in the still water. His hair was tangled and stuck up on odd directions, his beard was tangled, and he had lines near his eyes that he did not remember seeing before. Taking time, he washed his hands and then wet his hair and beard, combing them with his fingers.

He heard Nina moving around behind him. Looking back, he saw that she was putting the goose over the fire to roast.

"Thank you, Nina," Oli said.

He noticed that his knife was stuck into the side of the log. Nina pulled the knife loose and looked over at Oli.

Holding his hands in front of him, Oli stepped away. "Take it easy, Nina. Put the knife down."

Leaving the goose to roast, she walked downstream, knife in hand. Oli debated whether he should try and take the knife back. He could hear her cutting something, so she was not running. Nina came back with a bundle of thin, long branches in one hand and some weedy- looking things in the other.

Setting the bundle down, she walked to the roasting goose and rubbed it with the weeds. Oli decided that they must be herbs. Sitting back near the bundle, Nina started to weave a cone-shaped cage. She was using strips of bark to tie the branches together.

Nina made three of the cones. She walked along the stream, dropping a cone near pools as she passed. She then set a cone on the bottom of each pool, pounding a stake through the ends to prevent the current from washing them downstream.

Oli was in awe. She had just made three traps while he'd watched. Without a knife, she was not able to do so. Food just might not be a problem. While they sat eating the goose, he heard thunder to the west.

The second goose was every bit as good as the first. The meat offered fats which many of the leaner game did not have. Oli spent part of the day carving a crude spoon. He then warmed water in the rock dip and used the spoon to sip the hot liquid. It felt good having the warm water running down his throat.

He knew that he should be hunting, but Nina had walked upstream after eating and had not come back. He began to worry. If she was gone, so be it. If she was in trouble, he did not like that idea.

Walking in the direction in which she had gone, Oli searched, hoping to find her. He heard water splashing. Walking around the bend, he saw Nina in the water, her body naked and her wet dress drying on a bush.

Nina gasped, "Auugus!" when she saw him standing there.

Oli turned quickly. "I am sorry, Nina. I was not thinking."

He hurried back to the camp with the vision of her slender, naked body in his mind. The water had beaded on her skin, glistening on the soft curves. Oli stomped as he walked, pulling his hat off and then putting it back on roughly.

"You should be ashamed, Oli. She is not that kind of woman," he scolded himself.

Back at camp, he picked up his bow and walked out onto the plain to hunt, with the sound of the loose sole slapping with every step.

It was late when Oli returned to the camp. Cumulus clouds were building up in the west. Occasionally they heard thunder. Nina was sitting on the log with two catfish. He handed her the knife and she began to clean them. They would be breakfast.

Oli noticed a cook pot made of bark steaming on the edge of the fire. Nina had put bits of goose they'd saved along with some greens she had found and made a nice-smelling soup. Oli moved the bark container closer to the fire.

"Auugus!" Nina scolded as she moved it back.

He had noticed that the bark had started to char above the water level. Nodding, he realized that as long as the fire was below the water, the bark would not burn. Oli had a quiet and uncomfortable supper. His emotions were confusing. He washed up at the stream and then crawled into the shelter. Nina remained at the fire, staring out toward the darkening plain.

Oli awoke during the night. It was raining. Large drops were coming through the roof. Looking over, he could see that Nina was getting wet. Gently, he spread the deerskin coat out and covered her.

The crash of thunder woke him just as it was getting light. He sat up and watched the rain come down. He could smell the musky smell of Nina beside him. For an hour he watched the storm. Nina sat up and looked out.

They spread the deerskin coat out above them to keep the rain penetrating the roof, off them. Nina handed Oli one of the fish. Anticipating the storm, Nina had cooked it while they had the fire. He munched the fish, removing one of the many fish bones from his mouth.

He looked at the saturated ashes. The fire was gone. He sure hoped that Nina had the ability to start another when the rain stopped.

Nina suddenly got up and hurried to the stream. She was pulling the fish traps up from the bottom. One had a nice, fat catfish in it. She was chattering at him in a language he could not understand. Dragging the traps, she tossed the bow and spear towards Oli.

"Auugus!" She waved for him to follow.

Picking up the bow, his arrows, and the spear, Oli followed her up the bank and towards a knoll with a gnarled oak. They found some protection from the rain under the oak. Oli stuck his spear into the ground and draped the deerskin coat over the two of them.

It was midday when the rain stopped. Oli could see the stream churning and running over its banks. The peninsula now looked like a pond. While they sat waiting for the rain to stop, Nina started talking and drawing in the dirt. He recognized that she was telling him what had happened to her and how she'd gotten here.

She drew some domes, her village, and then several figures on the edge. She motioned that they had grabbed her. She continued the story for an hour. Afterwards, Oli sat back thinking about what she had described.

A war party had grabbed her and carried her off from her village. They had brought her west, leading her like a dog. Each night she'd been tied up with the stock, also stolen from the village. Somewhere along the way they had met some trappers, or others, who'd traded whiskey for some of the horses.

While the war party was drunk, she had slipped her bonds and escaped. She had been running for days as they hunted for her. She had eluded them and continued trying to get back to her village. Unable to find adequate food, she had collapsed at the spot he had found her. She had managed to start the fire for warmth.

Nina had said the name of the tribe that had taken her. Oli recognized it as the Cheyenne. She had referred to her village as Ho-Chunk. He did not recognize that name. He started to tell her his story, but quickly gave up. He just did not have the knack for drawing pictures and telling a story.

With the rain finished, Oli cut some more strips from the bottom of the deerskin coat and tied the fish traps together, making them easier to carry. They continued east, keeping to the low land and more or less following the swollen stream.

It was flowing west to the Missouri River. Oli shook his head, west was not the direction in which he dared to go. The couple days of rest and food had done both Nina and him good. They made good time walking east. An hour before sunset, Oli saw a grassy bank near the stream. It had some cottonwood trees to one side.

He started pulling some of the small brush into a dome shape. Weaving some branches in it, he then tossed leaves and twigs on top to make it more weather tight. Oli smelled smoke. Looking over, Nina was setting down a stick and blowing on some tinder laying on a piece of wood. Soon, she had a fire going and started broiling the fish.

She moved over to the stream and set the traps into a pool. Oli put a layer of leaves inside the shelter. Sharing the fish from the morning catch, they sat watching the fire as the darkness settled in. The new shelter was smaller. As they went to sleep, sharing the deerskin coat, both were careful to keep space between them. Sometime during the night Oli awoke, feeling Nina against him. The night was cold and they needed to keep warm.

A week later, while continuing east, Nina spotted some deer browsing on a side hill.

She called softly, "Auugus."

She motioned him to wait near the edge of some trees with the bow. She then slipped around the hill and slowly moved toward the deer. Seeing her, they moved toward Oli. When one was about 30 feet from him, he let an arrow fly. The deer jumped to the side and collapsed.

Together, Nina and Oli skinned and butchered the deer. She scraped the hide while he used pieces to repair his shoes. He unraveled more wool from his shirt and stitched the new soles on. He knew that the tops would not last too much longer, but he would deal with that when it happened.

Nina cut pieces of the hide and fashioned some moccasins. The rest of the hide was used as a leg cover at night. Oli knew that the green hide would not make durable soles for his boots. He figured that it was better than walking on his socks.

He had cut more off the bottom of the coat to make bags. As they collected edible plants, or dried fish, they put them into the bags for future use. His knee-length deerskin coat was now a waist coat. Oli was careful to save any thread as he shortened the coat. Some was used to sew up the bags. The rest he rolled up and stored in the ledger. This was kept in a pocket he had fashioned in the inside front of the coat.

It was late spring, or early summer, and game was plentiful. They kept the hides of any animals they killed and Nina made a decent cover out of them. The days were warm, but the nights could be quite chilly.

While traveling, they had less time to hunt or fish. Oli looked at their bags. Their food was depleted. They were finding more clusters of trees harboring game, on the plain. He decided that they needed to stop so they could hunt and fish for a time.

Nina put the fish traps into a small stream, while Oli began building a shelter. The sun was staying long in the sky, so Oli figured that it must be sometime in June. There was a grove of cedar. Pulling the tops together, it made a perfect shelter.

Nina came over and started cutting cedar boughs, weaving them into the walls and roof. They put a thick layer of boughs on the floor for sleeping comfort. Over this was spread a hide blanket that Nina had made. The money belt was stored near the edge, under the cedar boughs.

With a fire going, Oli walked out onto the plain with his bow. He heard turkeys gobbling. The sound still brought a chilling memory of the Indian attack. He was able to get close enough to shoot a nice tom. Walking back into camp with the turkey, Nina rushed up to get the bird. He sat and watched her pluck and clean the turkey. He figured that he could get used to this.

With the turkey roasted and eaten, and the camp in good order, they watched the sunset. As they headed to the shelter, Oli stopped and washed up. As he made his way to the shelter, Nina held the hide blanket open for him. He could see her soft skin in the fire light. Climbing into the bed, Oli hesitated for a moment. Nina reached over and pulled him over to her. Slowly she removed his clothes.

The sounds of their love added to the chorus of the, wolves, owls, frogs, and crickets that shared the night. Each with a purpose to find food or a mate. The morning chorus of the robins, warblers, blue birds, and others awoke Oli just as the sun was rising. If nature had allowed, he would have never left the soft woman beside him.

Wearing only his pants, he walked away from the camp through the dew covered grass to relieve himself. The experience of the night before had left him more alive than he could ever remember. The morning sun was brighter. The air fresher. He wanted to shout, but feared that he would awaken Nina.

Hurrying back, he was disappointed to see that she had gotten up and was going to the stream to bathe. Oli built up the fire to make their breakfast. He hummed a tune his mother used to sing when he was a child. He had not thought about his mother or family in a long time.

Oli knew he should be continuing east, but he was in no hurry to leave this place. He took the ledger from the deerskin coat. Using the good knife, Oli pried the emblem off the front. Using a narrow strip of leather from the coat, he made a necklace for Nina. When she came back from her bath, he presented the necklace to her.

"Auugus," she squealed and wrapped her arms around his neck.

The next few days they spent time catching and drying fish. Strawberries were ripe and plump on the knolls. Time was spent eating and enjoying the sweet fruit. Nina found some cattail roots and baked them on the edge of the fire, giving some variety to their diet.

One evening, she trimmed his hair and beard using the good knife. Oli looked at this reflection in the stream. His hair still long, but he looked groomed.

Most evenings she spent time quietly on a project. If he came near, she would shoo him away. They always watched the sunset together, and then sat around the fire drinking a hot brew that Nina provided.

While hunting, Oli could see the timber-covered hills to the east. Soon, they would have to continue on.

CHAPTER THIRTEEN

Oli slept in, enjoying the warmth of the hide blankets. Nina was already up. Crawling out of the shelter, he did not see her. No doubt she was out collecting something to eat for breakfast. He added some wood to the fire that had burnt down.

He dressed slowly and thought about his future. He knew that he did not want to lose Nina. He kept busy around the camp, looking up occasionally, watching for her to return. Oli sat on a log near the fire. The sun was telling him that it was late morning. Something was wrong!

Oli took his bow and started walking east along the stream. About 100 yards up, he saw a sandy area next to the stream where she had knelt down to take a drink. Finding this confirmed that this was the direction she had taken this morning. He continued slowly, finding evidence that he was still on her trail.

On a side hill covered with strawberries, he found a small basket that Nina had made from reeds. It was half full of berries. He slowly circled the area, finding additional moccasin tracks. He figured that there were about eight in the group.

All the tracks led northeast, toward the timber. Oli knew that he would not be returning to their camp, so he ran back and collected everything of value that could be easily carried. In his haste, he did not notice the deerskin shirt and breeches Nina had planned to surprise him with. He took care to put out the fire and cover the ashes with sand.

Oli's stomach was tight with fear. Had the Cheyenne caught up with them and grabbed her again? Had another war party taken her? The tracks were easy to follow, leading him to the timber. He could not read any struggle in the tracks. This gave him hope.

The group had stopped, just inside the timber, and had stood around in what apparently had been a discussion. Had they been deciding what to do with Nina? The sun was going down. Oli was concerned that he might lose the trail in the low light.

Curling up at the base of a tree, he slept. His dreams brought no comfort. He would see something through the woods and rush to it. He would find Nina's lifeless body. He would awake, drenched with sweat. Oli would then be chilled in the night air. The night was long and anything but restful.

With the sun coming up, Oli took some dried fish from the bag. He then realized that she must have one of the bags. He had only found one when he'd gone back. Oli stood and began to work out the trail again.

Something moved to his right. Looking up, he saw a brave with a raised spear rushing towards him. He threw himself to the left and the Indian brushed by, narrowly missing him with the spear. Leaping back to his feet, Oli faced his attacker. The brave whirled around and the two men faced each other.

"Where is Nina?" Oli shouted.

The brave brought the spear back to throw. Oli moved too slowly and the spear cut along his hip. He went down on one knee, his arm flashed forward, sending the good knife into the chest of the attacker. The Indian stepped forward and collapsed into a twisted heap.

The good knife had found its mark. Rolling the young brave onto his back, he stared into the cold eyes.

Wondering about Nina's fate, Oli snapped, "What tribe are you from?"

Struggling for breath, the young brave growled, "Ho-Chunk."

As he watched the life fade out of the young brave's body, the realization that he had just killed a man hit him. Oli felt the blood drain out of his face, he felt sick. He had never knowingly killed anyone before.

Now the young brave's sightless eyes stared at the sky. And to compound his anguish, it turned out that Nina had not been captured by an enemy. She had been found by her tribe. No doubt they were taking her home. She must have led the braves away from him, to protect him. He had now killed a member of the tribe.

Sadness swept over him. Whatever he'd hoped to have with Nina could not happen now. The burning in his hip brought Oli's attention back to the fact that he was wounded during the fight. He could feel the blood running down his leg. A quick inspection told him that it was a clean cut and not life-threatening.

Using his neckerchief, he folded it into a pad and then, taking his belt, he secured it in place. The shock of the wound was wearing off and it began to ache. Knowing that he could not stay there long, Oli's brain was racing.

He did not want to leave the brave lying there at the mercy of wolves or coyotes. He erected a quick platform and lifted the young brave's body onto it. This would prevent animals from ravaging the body before he was found. Placing the body into a peaceful position, Oli laid the spear alongside the body.

Oli removed the darning needle from the ledger. He removed his makeshift bandage and, using some thread saved in the ledger, he stitched the wound closed. He was sweating and feeling faint by the time he was done. Rinsing the neckerchief in a spring he found, he reapplied it to the wound.

Oli looked at the needle. He walked over and placed it on top of the brave's chest. He hoped that this would be recognized as a valued gift. Maybe they would understand that he respected the young brave. It was time to go.

Traveling quickly, Oli headed in an easterly direction. It was fully dark when he finally stopped to rest. He sat against an oak tree and looked at the stars. He thought back to the attack.

He could not remember reaching for the good knife. It had been total reflex. Was he that quick, or was he just lucky? The wound had started bleeding again. It was swollen and warm. Oli collected sap from the blisters of a balsam tree and spread it over the stitched wound. He then covered it with cobwebs.

It had worked for Nina, and he hoped that it would work on his wound. After rinsing the blood from his neckerchief, Oli went back under the oak tree. He sat and listened to the night sounds. He was alone again. This time it was different. This time he not only felt alone, but hurt inside at the loss of someone special.

He didn't know when it was, but he dozed off. When he awoke, Oli was lying on his side and the sun was just about to come up. He was damp from the dew. His hip was feeling somewhat better. Looking inside the bag, he had food for only a couple days. In his haste, Oli did not take the fish traps and he had not learned how to make fire from Nina.

He knew that he was only a couple weeks from the Mississippi River, and that steamships were traveling up and down the river. There had been much talk and excitement when the steamships would proceed north of St. Louis.

Oli's thoughts went back to Nina. He looked down at his tattered clothing. He thought about his first meeting with Nina. His beard and hair were long and blond. He must have looked every bit a wild man.

He continued east until he reached a stream. He saw a cave just off the water, in a rocky ledge. Oli looked into the cave and was greeted with the strong stench of skunk. Sitting on the bank of the stream, he looked around for anything to eat.

He walked in a circle, looking for food. There was thunder rumbling to the west. Looking up, he could see thunder heads forming. He found a large clearing where the trees had been blown down from a severe storm. He could see berry bushes covered with fruit. Oli did not recognize the raspberries, but he found them very tasty.

He heard some grunting and snorting. Looking over, he saw a young bear also enjoying the berries. More hungry than fearful, Oli moved further across the clearing and continued eating. He figured that the bear could have the east side and he would eat the west side. With his stomach full, Oli looked around and could not see the bear anywhere. A warm breeze began to pick up. It felt good, and smelled fresh with the oncoming rain.

Oli sat against a windfall and rubbed his satisfied stomach. Having slept poorly the past couple nights, Oli quickly dozed. Again, he was dreaming of sitting around the fire. The smoke was blowing in his face. His eyes opened and he was surrounded by smoke. It was a forest fire!

Lightning must have started the fire. Remembering the stream and the cave, Oli ran east, trying to locate them in the smoke. He found the stream and located the rock ledge. He could hear the roar of the flames coming his way. Oli was able to see the cave opening through the smoke. He ducked inside the cave and stopped in horror.

He was face to face with the bear. If he went out, the fire would get him. If he stayed, he feared that the bear would. Something was wrong with the young bear. Oli could smell burnt hair over the skunk smell. The bear lay all the way inside the cave and softly growled at him, but it did not move his way. It was favoring its right side.

Oli sat just inside the opening and hugged his knees. He could hear the snapping and crackling as the fire swept by.

"Too much fire," he grumbled.

Several uncomfortable hours were spent by the two cave dwellers, surrounded by the skunk odor. The bear stared at Oli and panted. He stared at the bear and wondered how long it would let him sit there before the closeness became too much. The night passed slowly, with Oli clutching his bag with very little food and his bow with three arrows.

He woke with a start, not realizing that he had dozed. Oli was looking at the bear standing in the back of the cave, growling and scratching at the dirt. No doubt the bear was going to leave whether he was in the way or not. Oli moved out of the cave.

He was shocked by what he saw. Yesterday, this area was green and lush with birds singing, chipmunks playing. Now it was charred and smoldering. The rain had held off, but the sky still looked angry. Oli stepped away from the opening. The bear moved out of the cave. Stopping, it sniffed the air. Oli saw the reason why the bear was so docile: There was a large burnt patch on the right hip. The bear moved past him and lumbered downstream.

He looked at the stream. There were dozens of dead fish floating on the ash-covered surface. Oli decided that they were recently dead fish and should be good to eat. Wading into the stream, Oli tossed several onto the shore. Then he collected smoldering sticks and got a fire going. He broiled the fish over the fire and ate his fill. Oli decided that while he had eaten better fish before, he was no longer hungry. He watched the bear scoop dead fish from the stream, then sit on the bank and eat them.

It was time to check the wound on his hip. It was healing nicely. He dipped his neckerchief into the stream and then heated it on the rocks next to the fire. Then he bathed the area. Oli figured that the hip wouldn't prevent travel. He needed to add to his provisions, so he collected several of the fish and began to dry them over the smoky fire.

As he watched the fish drying, he withdrew the ledger. He adjusted the money belt and sat back.

1 wool shirt, 1 wool pant, 1 pair woolen sock, 1 not so long underwear, 1 pair boots, 1 belt, 1 good knife, 1 deerskin jacket, 1 hat, 1 neckerchief, 1 bow, 3 arrows, food for one week (fish)

He had to be realistic. While he had a full set of clothes, they were in very poor condition. There was a good possibility that he would walk right out of his clothes and boots. He now thought about the hide cover he had left in the earlier camp. It would be handy right now to make some new pants and work on his shoes.

Oli walked up and down the stream, trying to decide his future. He should head for Leominster and buy the farm. The gold that he had in his money belt would accomplish that. He knew that losing his life was not worth trying to go back for the rest of the gold. He thought about going to St. Louis. His memories were muddy streets, a dirty stream, and an arrogant clerk. And then there had been Bart, who had turned out to be okay. He didn't have any desire to end up in St. Louis.

He continued to ponder his next move until the fish were dried. He put them into the bag and placed it inside the cave. He didn't want to take a chance, in case the rain started. Rubbing his nose, he hoped that the skunk odor wouldn't taint the fish.

Oli noticed a marshy area upstream. While they were not great eating, he decided to dig some cattail roots. He could pack them in mud and bake them next to his fire. Glancing at the sun, he estimated that there were two hours of light left. Adding some wood to the fire, Oli headed for the marsh.

After about 30 minutes, he had a nice pile of roots. He put them inside his coat and tied the sleeves together. Swinging the bundle onto his back, he wound his way back to the cave, looking at the results of the fire. Some areas were charred and others were hardly touched, no doubt evidence of a fast-moving fire.

Arriving at the cave, Oli was greeted by snorting and grunting. The bear was in the cave enjoying his fish! Dropping his bundle, he looked for the biggest rocks he could handle. Throwing them into the opening and shouting, Oli was able to send the young bear running downstream. Panic rising, he crawled into the cave. The bag was in shreds and all but bits of the fish had been eaten.

Emerging from the cave, Oli had fire in his eyes. Grabbing the bow, he looked for the bear. He had only one objective: Replace the fish with the young bear. Running downstream, he searched for any sign of the animal. He stopped, gasping for air. Raising his fist, he let out a rolling string of Finnish curses at the departed bear.

He realized that the bow with heat-tempered wooden arrows was not the way to bring down a bear, young or old. As he walked back to the cave, drops of rain started hitting his face. Throwing one more curse in the bear's direction, he ran back to the cave.

Oli moved his fire to the ledge under an overhang. He was able to dig a pocket to protect the fire even more from the rain. As insurance, he leaned slabs of rock against the ledge on each side of the fire.

Sitting back, with the rain dripping off his hat, Oli smiled. "Not a bad little fireplace."

He only wished that he had time to put a roof over where he was sitting. Once he had a bed of coals, his only choice was the strong-smelling cave. Putting some extra wood onto the fire, Oli rolled the clay-covered roots on a piece of bark and went back to the cave to dine.

Oli awoke to a wet, gray morning. He had slept as close to the opening as possible. One for the fresh air, and two, to make sure that the bear noticed him if it came back. He crawled further inside to see if the bear had missed any of the fish. He was able to collect enough for a small breakfast.

He was pleased when he checked on the fire. There were plenty of coals buried in the ashes. He got the fire going and placed some more cattail roots to bake. Despite the gloomy morning, the air was fresh.

He needed to bolster his spirits. He remembered when his mother would clean the house from end to end to raise her spirits. He had no house to clean, but he could improve his wild man look. Selecting a proper stone, Oli sharpened the edge of his knife. Then, removing his clothes, he carefully washed them. He had to be careful. A proper scrubbing would leave them in rags. After draping them onto bushes, he washed himself from stem to stern.

Sitting naked on the stream's edge, Oli began cutting his wild hair and shaving his beard. He wetted his neckerchief and warmed it next to the fire. He used this to steam his beard to reduce the pulling as he shaved.

By midday Oli sat clean and dressed, breaking the clay off the cattail roots and feeling almost human. He knew that he had done a good job cleaning the clothes. The wool next to his skin was itching. When he looked into a calm pool in the stream, he was shocked at how much he had aged. His blue eyes looked so serious and his face was weathered.

It took three days to replace the fish that the young bear had eaten. Using the bow, Oli was able to get about one fish per hour. Then it took time to dry them. He made a bundle of the fish and some baked cattail roots in his coat. The sun was just coming up when he walked away from the cave. He felt clean and well-fed. Looking back, he saw the young bear sniffing around the area where he had cleaned the fish.

He called to the bear, "It's all yours, young bear. Keep it clean, in case I should ever return."

Chuckling, Oli stepped out briskly. His mother was right, there was nothing like being clean.

* * *

Rain! For a week straight, it had rained. Oli's shoes had come apart and he finally had to abandon them. His woolen socks had become so full of holes that they also had to be removed. Walking barefoot, he had to be careful where he stepped. His clothes were now sodden, and sour. His hat was his only shelter.

Huddled underneath a spreading oak tree, Oli ate the last of his food. He knew that in the next day or two he would be back to eating raw meat. He looked up and saw stars. Maybe the rain was over.

Oli walked through the forest. The sky was getting lighter, with the promise of the sun breaking through. His thoughts drifted to the past year. He now realized how ill-equipped he had been for the trip. Even though he'd had supplies and a horse when he'd left the wagon train, he now felt more capable of surviving in the wilderness. He could get food with nothing more than a knife, could read sign, and could defend himself. Most important, being alone in the wilderness was not scary. It was comfortable.

Even as miserable as he felt, he now looked forward to a new day's challenge. Sunshine welcomed him in the morning. Oli sat next to the oak, soaking up the warmth. His hung his pants and shirt to dry. He was worried about his feet. They were bruised and cut from walking barefoot. His coat was not needed to carry food, so he cut half of each sleeve off and made a crude pair of moccasins.

For two days, he walked east. Berries were plentiful, so he was not going hungry. It was just before dark when he spotted a ruff grouse roosting in an aspen. Oli slowly crept closer. A well placed rock knocked the bird out of the tree. Flapping and running, the bird did its best to get away. Oli ran, ducking under low branches, and caught the bird. A quick, snapping motion of his wrist dispatched it.

Sitting back and admiring the catch, he suddenly froze. He had heard something. It was talking or arguing. Civilization! Tucking the head of the bird under his belt, he moved towards the sound. He came up to a river.

On the other side, he could see a girl arguing with two young men. One of the men was trying to convince the girl to accompany him to something the next day. Oli could not move for a moment. She was stunning, with shoulder-length blond hair. Without realizing it, Oli had waded across the river and stood on the bank 30 feet away.

He heard himself say, "She does not want to go with you."

All three of them looked at him, startled by the unexpected stranger. A quick appraisal from the two men told them that there was nothing to fear from the ragtag bum who had climbed out of the river.

The quiet one walked up to Oli. "I'm Jake Wolfe, and that is my brother Tate. You best move along. We don't take kindly to trash like you stopping in Pony Hollow."

"All I said is the lady does not want to go with your brother. You should respect her wishes."

The swing came low and fast and hit Oli in the middle of his money belt. Stumbling back, Oli sat down hard. Catching his breath, he leaped to his feet. Jake was holding a broken wrist. He had expected to hit an unprotected mid-section, but had struck gold instead.

Tate moved quickly towards Oli. "What did you do to my brother?"

Moving around him, Oli sized him up. Tate was a big one. "He swung at me. Your brother tried to throw a surprise punch at me, and it did not work out."

Oli saw him slip the thong off his side arm. "If your hand touches the grip of your gun, I will put a knife in your chest before you can clear leather." Oli's voice was cold and clear.

Tate stopped with his hand hovering over his weapon. He didn't know whether Oli had a knife or not. "If I didn't have to get Jake to the doctor, I would deal with you right now. Like Jake said, you best move on," Tate said, then turned to his brother and headed for town, the young lady forgotten.

"You did not have to do that. I could have handled it."

It took Oli a moment to realize that she was talking to him. His focus was on the two men disappearing into the distance.

"Did you hear me?" she said.

"I am sorry, miss. It has been a long time since I have heard so many words spoken. I am sure you could have. It just is not in my nature to hear men talk to ladies that way."

"Well, how about that, a gentleman in rags, appearing right out of the river." She looked skeptically at him.

Oli began to straighten his clothes, and then gave up. "My name is Oli August. What town is this?" he asked.

"You are in Pony Hollow and just walked out of the Turkey River," she responded.

Oli sat down on the bank of the river. "What brought you out here this time of evening?"

"I love this time of the evening. I often walk along the river, listening to the frogs and night birds. That is why the Wolfe brothers knew they could find me here."

The sun was large in the western sky as it moved toward the horizon. A breeze sprung up, rustling the aspen tree leaves. The lady pulled her wrap tighter around her shoulders.

"What was it that they wanted you to join them for?" Oli inquired.

Furling her brow, she looked at him. "Why, the 4th of July celebration. You did know it was the 4th tomorrow, didn't you?"

"I'm sorry, I did not. I have just finished several months in the West. I was pretty much lost and out of contact with anyone. As you can see, I need to purchase clothing. I also need to send a message to a family in Pennsylvania."

"Pennsylvania?" she asked.

"I met a man named Don Sikes last winter. I buried him in the spring and promised to let his family know. I guess you could say he was a friend. He helped me through a long winter."

Stepping back, she took a closer look at the man in rags. He was thin. His hips were narrow and his shoulders broad. His blond hair needed combing and he needed a shave. She was looking into the bluest eyes she could remember.

Feeling uncomfortable with the pause in the conversation, Oli stood up and tossed a stone into the river.

Searching for something to say, he asked, "You wouldn't have a flint, would you? I need to start a fire and cook this bird. I also need to clean up a bit."

Oli knew that he couldn't enter town looking like he did. He had noticed a pot that had been used for target practice lying not far from him. He could plug the holes with wooden plugs and heat water to wash up and shave.

The blond lady reached into her pocket and brought out a flint. "Here you are. You can return it to me tomorrow during the celebration. The store, barber, and bath house will be open in the morning."

Oli caught his breath for a moment and looked into her hazel eyes. Did she say tomorrow at the celebration?

His heart began to beat a bit faster. "I will do that."

With a smile, she twirled her dress as she turned. "I have to go now. It was a pleasure meeting you, Mr. August. Oh, my name is Joan Maier."

Watching her walk away with the setting sun shining on her golden blond hair, Oli called out, "Until tomorrow then, Miss Maier."

Sitting back down with his coat over his shoulders and a smile so big that it hurt his face, Oli stared at the river. "You have found your gold, Oli."

CHAPTER FOURTEEN

Oli sat on the bank next to his small fire. The pot had been plugged and the water was steaming. The bird hung on two green willow sticks and was dripping juice onto the coals as the grouse browned.

Finding a piece of flat stone, he worked the edge of the knife blade, planning on shaving and trimming his shoulder-length hair. Using the fire light, he tore pieces from the bird and stripped the meat from its bones with his teeth.

Hunger had driven him to eat it while the meat was still on the rare side. The bloody juice ran down his chin, soaking the heavy whiskers. He wished that he had some coffee. He could have asked the girl, but he feared that she would laugh at him and leave.

First thing in the morning, he would go into town and get cleaned up. At the mercantile, he would buy new clothes. He would then find Joan Maier and give her back the flint. He hoped that she wouldn't be in a hurry to leave, so the two of them could visit a bit.

This would be the first July 4th celebration he had a chance to attend. He tried to think of where he had been last year on that date, but everything ran together and he couldn't be sure. He wondered if it would be like midsummer celebration back in Finland, with food and drink, folk dancing, and a large bonfire at midnight.

He was washing his hands and rinsing his face when he caught sight of someone coming his way, carrying a lantern. The light danced off bushes, and the grass as it swung. Oli thought about all of the conveniences that were available when you lived with other people and had stores. These, and so many other things folks took for granted.

Standing up and shaking the water from this hands, Oli walked over to meet the man. "Stay where you are," a stern voice ordered him. There was the sound of a hammer being cocked.

"Am I doing something wrong?" Oli asked. "If this is private property, I will put out the fire and leave."

The man stopped a few feet away, holding the lantern high. The light reflected off a badge on the man's shirt and his pockmarked face. "Drop your knife on the ground where I can see it."

Oli's heart suddenly began to pound under his ragged shirt. "My name is Oli August and I have spent months in the wilds. I just found your town this evening."

"Don't make me shoot your scrawny carcass!" the man growled. "You got two seconds to drop the knife or I will fire!"

Oli reached for the good knife and dropped it onto the ground near the fire. The lawman waved him back with the barrel of the gun and scooped up the knife. He then tipped the pot of hot water onto the fire with the toe of his boot.

"Now, keep your hands up and walk ahead of me," he was instructed.

The tattered man walked slowly, wondering if he should take a chance and run. The problem was, where could he run to? He had found a town, but it might be miles to the next one. He would be running with nothing to survive with, not even a knife. He would be a hunted man.

Oli was sure that he would be able to explain that arresting him was a mistake once he got to the jail. He could feel the weight of the money belt around his waist. He suddenly feared that it could be taken from him. How could he explain having the old Spanish coins?

The dusty street of Pony Hollow had several clapboard covered buildings on each side. Several had lamps or lanterns on the porches, giving Oli a glimpse of the bunting and other decorations in preparation for the next day.

He was told to stop in front of a brick and stone building. The lawman turned a key in the door and pushed it open. He then gave Oli a shove as they walked in. The sign on the outside said: Sheriff's Office.

Standing, waiting for the cell to be opened, he looked around. A rack with three rifles was on the wall next to a small stand with a tin basin. A mirror hung above the stand. An oak desk sat in the middle of the front room. Two chairs went with the desk. A cot was against the wall next to the desk. A single cell was at the back of the building.

Oli said, "There is some mistake, Sheriff. I just walked out of the wilderness and couldn't have done anything wrong . . ."

"Save it for the judge," the sheriff said, cutting him off. "Whatever you have under that shirt, give it to me."

A burning flash went through Oli's stomach. He decided that he'd best let the lawman know what he had. "I have the gold that I found in the western mountains, my ledger, and the sheath for my knife."

"Gold, huh?" the sheriff snorted. "Put everything on the desk."

Carefully opening the shirt, he removed the money belt and put it onto the desk. It thumped as he set it down. He then laid the ledger and knife sheath next to the belt.

The sheriff motioned for him to go into the cell. As Oli walked pass the mirror, he saw his reflection. He hardly recognized the undernourished, hollow-eyed face looking back at him.

Again, the sheriff shoved him when he entered the cell too slowly. There was a set of narrow bunks against the left wall and a barred window high on the back wall. The barred door clanged shut behind him.

"There's a chamber pot for you in the cell and I got a bucket of water out here if you're thirsty," the lawman informed him.

Oli turned around and put his hands on the bars. The sheriff was hefting the money belt. "You say these come from the mountains. I always wanted to see the Rockies."

An old keyed safe sat below the front window. The lawman knelt down, put the belt and ledger in and locked it. He hung the leather sheath with the good knife on a peg on the wall, and then looked at the ragged man in his cell.

"When I get a chance, I'm going to send out some telegrams and find out where you stole the gold. Ain't no way you'd be walking in rags with this kind of fortune." The sheriff stuck the key into his pocket checked the coffee pot on the potbelly stove. He poured himself a cup and sat behind his desk.

"You wouldn't have another cup of coffee, would you?" Oli asked.

"Nope, this was the last one," the sheriff replied. "Come morning I will make another pot and you'll get breakfast."

Reaching through the bars, Oli filled the dipper from the bucket and, pressing his face to the bars, he drank. He was worried. He had no way to prove who he was or if the gold was his. Those who could confirm he had been to the Rockies were in Oregon. The boarding house in Boston had had no idea where he was going.

Tom Franklin came to mind. He would be trapping in the mountains. Oli sat on the bunk and held his head in his hands. Just an hour ago he had been thinking of being married to Joan. He snickered, marry him? Just like the sheriff, she didn't know him from Adam.

The door opened and a young man dressed in a green wool shirt and dark wool pants entered. He hung his round-crowned hat on the peg next to Oli's knife sheath. "Sorry I'm late, Ben. I kind of had my eyes on Lilly at the dance and forgot the time."

"You best keep track of the time, Keller. I don't need a deputy that keeps me from my supper," the sheriff said, scolding the young lawman.

"It won't happen again, sheriff." the young man replied, checking on the coffee pot. Seeing that it was empty, he tossed the grounds into the slop pail. Ben handed Keller the coffee cup and that was also dumped.

Oli sat on the bunk, watching the brown liquid splash along the lip of the pail, some hitting the floor. Seeing the brew wasted and sitting in the cell was almost enough to make him cry.

"Who we got in the cell?" Deputy Keller asked.

"Just some trash that was down by the river threatening people. He'll be staying with us until the judge comes the day after tomorrow."

Oli's eye grew large, the sheriff was talking about the two men that he'd had a confrontation with down by the river. That was why he'd known about the knife!

Crossing to the cell door, he grabbed the bars. "Sheriff! Those men attacked me! I never touched them!"

Waving a finger at Oli, the lawman said, "If I hear another word from you, I will put a knot on your head that will keep you quiet until morning. You will get a chance to tell it to the judge."

The sheriff grabbed his hat off his desk and clamped it onto his head. "See you in the morning, Chet."

The door slammed behind the lawman. Oli stood holding the bars, feeling helpless. The young lawman walked over to have a look at him. "Sheriff Tomson doesn't have much patience with prisoners. You best keep quiet until you see the judge. The most you'll probably get is 30 days and an invite to leave town. What's your name?"

"It's Oli. Oli August," he replied, dropping his arms to his sides and turning toward the bunk.

"If I make a pot of coffee, would, you be interested in a cup?" the deputy asked.

Turning around Oli replied, "Yes! Yes, I would."

Sitting on his bunk, Oli sipped the hot, dark brew. The truth was, he was out of the weather, had a bed off the ground to sleep on, a meal coming in the morning, and coffee. While he had lost his freedom for the moment, his situation was better than it had been in some time.

He looked across the room at the safe. Inside was his future, the reward for all the risks and pains he had endured. The safe was a heavy wooden cabinet with a cast iron door, and a clasp and lock.

Finishing his coffee, Oli called to the deputy, "I sure could use another cup, if you got it."

Chet Keller brought the pot over and filled Oli's cup, handing it back through the bars. He looked at the rags that the prisoner was dressed in. "It looks like you've been having some hard times for a while."

"Last year I took a wagon train out to the Rockies and just finished a long walk back. I can't say I expected this type of welcome once I found folks again," Oli said between sips of coffee.

"You should have made sure you had a horse, and if you went all the way out there and then come walking back, it don't make sense. I hope it wasn't because you forgot something," the deputy said, chuckling at his own joke as he put the pot back onto the stove.

Oli sat back on the bunk and whispered, "I had a horse, a good horse."

He removed the crude footwear made from the sleeves of his coat and placed them underneath the bunk. The bed was surprisingly comfortable. Lying beneath the clean blankets, Oli was soon asleep. The deputy sat at the desk, half dozing, with a newspaper open in front of him.

The next morning, as promised, a heavy-set woman brought in a pot of oatmeal. The deputy went to the wash stand and took out a tin plate and a spoon. "You ready for something to eat, Oli?"

The woman had sweetened the oatmeal with honey and had added some dried fruit. Oli ate two plates of the porridge and had two cups of coffee. Finishing the meal, the deputy washed the plates in the basin and then dumped the water into the slop pail.

"I got to empty this. I am going to let you out to empty your chamber pot, but don't try nothing funny," Deputy Keller said, patting the Colt Paterson on his hip. "I ain't never shot a man and don't want you to be my first."

They went out the back door of the jail. The town was bathed in sunshine. Oli could hear folks getting ready for the celebration along the main street. He walked ahead of the young deputy to a ditch near the outhouse. They emptied their waste into the ditch.

"Mind if I use the outhouse before going back in?" Oli asked. "I don't like using the pot."

Chet waited for Oli to relieve himself and then the two of them went back into the jail. The brief time in the sunshine had lifted the prisoner's spirits, but as the cell door clanged shut, the reality of his problems came back.

Throughout the day the sounds of the merriment outside filtered in through the barred window. Sheriff Tomson relieved the young deputy just before noon. He was carrying a wicker basket with fried chicken and sourdough biscuits. He also had a pail of beer.

"Don't figure you're going to get his kind of treatment in the coming days," he told Oli, "but the gals at the café thought I should bring it to you because it's a holiday."

The crisp chicken and beer tasted great. The sheriff left the front door open to watch the goings on. Shouts, laughter, and music drifted into the jail. Oli watched from his cell, hoping to catch a glimpse of Joan Maier. His hopes were not fulfilled.

As the day wore on, the festivities moved further out of town, with horse races, target shooting, and a rodeo. Deputy Keller came in around 6 PM and relieved the sheriff. He had packages with bread and meat for the evening meal.

Oli was still full from the large noon meal and set his package at the end of his bunk. He reached through the bars for the dipper and took some water from the bucket. The deputy looked over and told him, "I will be making coffee in a bit."

The small cell was beginning to close in on Oli. After months in the wide open spaces he needed to walk more than five steps from wall to wall. He laid on the bunk with his eyes closed and thought about the green valley, the cabin, nights with Nina, and the good horse.

"Coffee's ready," Chet called to him as he filled the mugs. Handing one to Oli, he told him, "You best eat the bread and meat before it gets dry on you."

The prisoner thanked him and sat on the bunk, chewing the meal and drinking coffee. Bored, the deputy pulled a chair in front of the cell and had his coffee there.

"What do the Rocky Mountains look like?" he asked. "I mean, are they as high as people say?"

Wiping his mouth with the back of his hand, Oli swallowed before speaking. "It is hard to describe. They reach up to the heavens, the, tops white with snow. You can't ride or walk right up to them. Smaller hills rise up before them, some almost as high as the peaks. The peaks rise up above the plain days before you get close."

"Everything is flat around here," Chet complained. "We got some trees and hills, but nothing like what you're talking about."

The men talked and drank coffee throughout the evening, while the sounds of the 4th celebration slowly dwindled. "You want to use the outhouse before going to sleep?" the deputy asked.

Oli didn't have to, but he wasn't going to miss a chance of getting out of the cell and getting some fresh air. He stepped out into the warm evening breeze. The stars stood out in the night sky.

He sat in the outhouse, curling his toes on the wooden floor. He thought about trying to make a break, for just a moment. He knew that he couldn't. He would be running away from the gold in the safe and just might get shot.

There was a rap on the door. "Hurry up in there. The skeeters are getting me."

As they walked back toward the jail, Oli prayed that he wouldn't have to spend a month in the small cell. He did have a witness to what had happened. Joan was there. He couldn't be sure that she would be allowed to, or even want to, speak on his behalf.

Once back inside the cell, he ran what had happened over and over in his mind. Had he provoked Jake Wolfe? He had also threatened Tate, but not before he'd made a move toward his gun. Would these acts go against him because he was an outsider? The way he was dressed wouldn't help, either.

Oli was slowly accepting the reality that he would be spending a month in the cell. When it was over he would have his gold and he would get far away from Pony Hollow. The deputy pulled his boots off and hung his holster on the peg above his bed before lying on the cot. Oli could hear the young man snoring as he himself fell asleep.

Suddenly, the door burst open and two men charged in. The shocked deputy uttered, "What the . . ." the taller of the two men cracked him over the head with a gun barrel as he tried to get up, dropping him like a poleaxed steer.

Startled, Oli sat up, hitting his head on the upper bunk. Dropping back to the mattress, the prisoner grabbed the top of his head, pain shooting through his skull. He looked out toward the office, trying to figure out what was going on.

He saw a man pointing a revolver at him. "Don't shoot that damn thing, Harry," the man behind him said. "You'll wake the whole town."

"Hell, it's just a rag of a man. Not even worth a bullet, Rex."

In the low light of the lantern, Oli could see the young deputy lying on the plank floor, blood running down the side of his head. Then panic filled him. The men knelt down in front of the safe and were breaking the lock. After several hits with a shoeing hammer, the lock gave way.

Digging through the safe, the men checked the ledger and then tossed it onto the floor. They pulled out the money belt. "Damn Harry, this thing is heavy," Rex hissed.

After finding nothing else of value inside the safe, the two men set the belt onto the desk. "Find the key and put the deputy in the cell," the tall man said.

Retrieving the key from the desk, they dragged the unconscious man in front of the cell. Oli stood near the bunk. "That belt is mine," he pleaded.

Opening the cell door, they tossed the deputy inside and relocked the door, dropping the keys onto the desk. "We'll take good care of it for you," Harry snorted at him.

Rex grabbed the belt and checked the front to make sure that the street was empty. Closing the door behind them, the two men were gone. Oli could hear the sounds of their departing horses.

Grabbing the iron bars of the window, he pulled himself up and shouted, "Help! I need help here! Help!"

His mind racing in desperation, Oli went to the deputy and began emptying his pockets onto the floor to see if he had another key for the cell. He saw the gaping wound on the young man's head.

"Damn, I think they killed you," he said, checking for signs of life. Oli knew that he had to stop the bleeding. He pulled the blanket off his bunk and wet the corner in the water bucket. He then sat holding the deputy's head in his lap and held pressure on the wound.

As he sat, his heart was pounding. Every second, the gold was getting farther away. Sitting in the middle of the cell, holding the young man, he continued to shout for help, his voice hoarse from the strain.

After what seemed like hours there was someone on the walk in front of the jail. Oli carefully put the deputy's head down, using the blanket for a pillow. The bleeding had stopped.

As he was getting up, the door opened. "Hey, Keller, who the hell has been yelling in here?" It was Sheriff Tomson.

"Son-of-a-bitch! What happened here?" the angry sheriff shouted. The safe stood open with its contents, less the money belt, scattered on the floor. He came to the cell and looked in.

"They hit your deputy and put him in here. Then they broke into the safe," Oli said, he voice croaking.

"And then you dug through his pockets!" the sheriff snapped. "Were you looking for coins to buy a bottle?"

Anger raged through Oli. If he could have gotten his hands on the sheriff at that moment, he would have strangled him and felt no regret. He couldn't believe that so many things could go wrong so fast, and the blockheaded sheriff wasn't seeing him as anything more than thieving trash.

Swallowing the angry words which could only get him in more trouble, Oli said, "Chet needs a doctor. I stopped the bleeding, but I don't know . . ."

The sheriff grabbed the keys and unlocked the cell. "Help me get him on the cot. You try anything and I'll shoot your worthless hide," he threatened.

Even though the deputy was still alive, he hung like dead weight as they carried him. Oli was put back into the cell and ordered to place the contents of the deputy's pockets near the water bucket.

The sheriff went after the doctor, leaving Oli in the silence of the brick and stone building. The pleasure of the coffee was long forgotten as he stared at the unmoving deputy lying on the cot. The names of Rex and Harry went through his mind. If it took the rest of his life, he would have a reckoning with them.

Oli sat in the shadows of the cell while the doctor worked on the injured man. The first light of morning was showing in the barred window. Sheriff Tomson sat at his desk drinking coffee. He had offered none to his prisoner.

The doctor spoke softly to the sheriff, shaking his head. Oli figured that it was bad news for the young deputy. With nothing else that he could do, he prayed for the deputy and a little for himself. His parents had always told him that it was wrong to pray for riches, so he prayed that the men who had stolen the gold had slow horses.

He laid on his bunk with his eyes closed, tired from the lack of sleep during the night. Oli didn't look at the woman, bringing in breakfast. She set it on the sheriff's desk and then exclaimed, "What happened to Chet?"

"The office was robbed last night," Sheriff Tomson told her.

"Robbed?" she replied. "There is nothing of value to rob in here."

"I took a money belt filled with gold off the troublemaker in the cell. I guess someone heard me talking about it and come and got it," Tomson explained.

The woman looked at the man lying on the bunk. "You arrested him?" she asked. "What for?"

"He attacked and threatened the Wolfe brothers," Sheriff Tomson replied.

"He did not! I was there, sheriff!" she snapped. "They were bothering me and he came to my defense. Jake hit him for no reason and Tate was going to pull a gun on him. He didn't do anything a gentleman wouldn't have done!" Joan Maier was mad clear through. By this time, Oli was sitting on the bunk, wide awake.

"I am sorry, Joan. That's what Tate told me," the sheriff said, defending his actions.

"And now, you tell me his money was stolen because you talked about having it in the safe?" If ever there was a man that didn't have a leg to stand on in front of an angry woman, it was the sheriff.

The sheriff's face was red and his eyes blazing as he got the key and opened the cell. Oli was no fool. Joan was making a better case than he could ever have. He just kept quiet. Standing in the middle of the jail, he was unsure of what to do.

Joan knelt beside the deputy and asked, her voice softer, "What did the doctor say?"

The sheriff cleared his throat before speaking. "He didn't give him much hope. He got an awful knock on the head."

"I want you to move him to my parents' house. My brother is gone with the army and we can put him in his room," she told Sheriff Tomson.

"When the doc comes back, I'll have him set it up," he told her.

"Who went after the robbers?" Joan asked.

Again, the sheriff found himself in a corner. "I have to get a posse together. We don't even know who it was."

"Ones was named Harry, he was tall and hit Chet. The other was Rex. He broke into the safe," Oli said.

Deflecting his anger onto Oli, he snapped, "You're telling me this now! The damn robbers will be out of the territory before you think to share who they are!"

"Sheriff Tomson. You gave me no opportunity to tell you. You knew I was in here when it happened, and all you thought was I was trying to steal from your deputy's pockets when I was looking for a key to the cell, so I could go get help," Oli replied, his blue eyes locked in angry stares with the sheriff.

Frowning, Joan said, "Of course, you didn't get a posse together. The stolen money was just the property of the man in rags that had challenged your friends, the Wolfes."

Attempting to change the course of the conversation, the sheriff requested, "Miss Maier, I would like you to stay with Chet until he can be moved." And then to Oli, he said, "You get out of my office and stay out of my sight. If we get your gold, it will be given back to you and then I expect you to leave town."

"I want to be part of the posse," Oli requested.

"What are you going to do, run alongside our horses and then throw rocks at the robbers?" he sneered

Her voice much sweeter than it had been before, Joan said, "Ben. Mr. August is just volunteering to go after his gold with you. Chet's gun is right here on the peg. He can ride one of my father's horses, and before you leave, he can use some of my brother, Martin's clothes."

Oli admired the way she handled the sheriff. Before he left the office, Oli gave her back the flint and thanked her for loaning it to him.

In the next hour he met Joan's mother and father, who looked upon him with distaste. The clothing fit close enough, right down to the boots. The light blue wool shirt and dark blue pants hung a bit loose on his underweight frame.

He had to poke another hole into the gun belt to keep it from falling off his hips. The good knife and sheath were back at the nape of his neck. Oli walked out onto the front porch and was pleased with the dun that her father had saddled for his use. There was a bedroll tied to the back of the saddle and saddle bags.

"I put a few things you might need in the bags," her father told him.

Oli tipped the flat-brimmed hat to Joan's parents as he rode away. He hadn't been so well-dressed since leaving the cabin. With the Colt on his right side and a possible bag on his left, he was ready to face Rex and Harry.

He rode up to the crowd of people outside the saloon. Sheriff Tomson stood on the porch, trying to get a posse together. "I tell you men, the town will pay $3 a day if you'll go after the robbers."

A man with a pot belly and suspenders to hold his pants up replied, "Those two are killers. Your posse pay ain't going to help us if we're dead."

Glaring at Oli, he growled, "It looks like it will be you and me. These damn buggers would rather suck down rye than go after the men that got your money."

The heavy set woman brought them two bags of food from the café. The men stuffed them into their saddle bags before riding off. Joan stood at the jailhouse door holding Oli's ledger, which had been lying on the floor. She had just finished glancing through some of the notes entered by the blond-haired man. As the two men galloped out of town she whispered, "Come back safe, Oli August."

As they rode, Oli learned more about the men who had robbed the gold. Harry Cole and Rex Harper had recently come into Pony Hollow. Word was that they had killed several men in New Orleans and were wanted men.

Sheriff Tomson had no flyers on them, so as far as he was concerned the men were living within the law. Dubuque, Iowa was a two-day ride south of Elkader and had steamboat service. If the men caught a steamboat on the Mississippi River, they would be gone, along with Oli's gold.

The robbers were six hours ahead of them. They would have been riding at night, which would be slower, and they might have stopped to rest a couple hours before daylight.

Oli asked the sheriff how he knew that the men were headed for Dubuque. Sheriff Tomson rode staring straight ahead for a couple of minutes, before answering. "My gut tells me, because that's where I would go. You had old coins in that belt. They're not something that can be sold or traded just anywhere without questions being asked. They can catch a boat to St. Louis, and there they'll find people that will melt them down or buy them to sell to collectors. These people won't ask questions, or talk."

The road they were riding on was covered with tracks from horses and wagons. "I don't see how we can be sure they went this way with all the tracks," Oli said.

"Their horses were tied alongside the jail. I got a good look at the tracks. If they pull off to water their horses or ride off to the side, I will recognize them," the sheriff replied.

The men kept their horses at a mile-eating trot and they followed the road to Dubuque. They stopped once when they met a freight wagon. The driver hadn't seen any riders, but had passed a smoldering campfire shortly after getting on this road. It was a couple of miles back.

Thanking the man, the two continued on, watching for the location of the fire. Oli saw the camping spot first. He got off the horse to stretch his legs. The sheriff swung down from his roan. After a brief search around the area, they climbed back onto the horses.

"This is their camp, alright," the sheriff confirmed. "They are about three hours ahead of us."

As they rode, Oli pulled the Colt, checking on the loads. He slipped the gun back into his holster. For a moment he thought he saw a look of approval on the sheriff's face. The men ate while they rode. Joan's father had put a canteen filled with water inside one of the saddle bags.

They rode into a small town in mid-afternoon. The sheriff stopped at the livery and made a deal to get fresh horses. While switching the saddles, they found out that the two men had been in the town and had bought a couple of bottles at the saloon.

The hostler had given the sheriff and Oli two plain-bred mustangs. He promised them that the horses would run all day and have something left for the night. The plan was to get their horses back on the return trip.

"They are only a couple hours ahead of us now," the sheriff told Oli. "They will pull off the road for the night and nurse the bottles. Right now, they may be figuring they got away."

Oli's legs and back were beginning to ache. He hadn't ridden much since being with the wagon train. Even then, it had not been the hard riding that they were doing now. He watched the sheriff sitting squarely on the other mustang, looking like he could go forever.

Shortly after dark, the sky clouded over and it began to rain. Sheriff Tomson pulled off the road underneath some oak trees. "We'll never see them in this weather. Let's grab some sleep and hope the storm blows over before morning."

Pulling the gear off the horses, they tied them to some low brush. Spreading their blankets under a large oak, Oli found that there was a rain slicker inside the bedroll. He covered the blanket with it to keep the rain off. Before turning in, the men ate a cold supper.

During the night, the storm blew through. Before daylight they were back on the road. The dry ground had absorbed the rain, and soon their horses were kicking up dust. Sheriff Tomson was riding slower and looking for the tracks of the riders ahead of them.

"There is a chance we might be ahead of them. We might have missed their camp while riding in the rain," the sheriff said.

All Oli could think was that they had to find them and get the gold back. His future depended on it. He remembered the looks on Joan's folk's faces when they'd seen him walk up. While Joan might see beyond the rags he was wearing, it might take the gold to make them accept him.

By this evening Harry and Rex would be in Dubuque. They could take any number of steamboats. The sheriff guessed that they would go south, but there were lots of towns they could disappear in to the north.

Riding beside the sheriff, Oli had gained confidence in the man's abilities. His disposition had not changed, but at least now his anger was directed at the robbers. The south breeze brought the smell of road dust to them. The sheriff pulled his mustang to a walk.

"Someone, or something, has moved ahead of us beyond the rocks. It was close enough that the dust hasn't settled," sheriff told him. "It could even be the wind picking up the dirt . . ."

The crack of a rifle pierced the mid-morning air. Oli spurred his horse toward an outcrop of rocks to his right. Leaping off the animal, he looked back for the sheriff. A jolt ran through him when he saw Tomson lying in the road.

"Son-of-a-bitch," he growled. Running back in a crouch, he reached the downed man and grabbed his arms. Again there was a shot that kicked up some dust down the road from them.

He heard the firing of a revolver as he dragged the wounded sheriff behind the rocks. He was thankful that the robbers' muzzle loaders provided only one shot and that he was out of effective range of the hand gun.

Gasping for breath, he sat against the sandstone outcrop. The sheriff had a bloody wound on his upper chest. The stunned man began to try to get up. Oli held him down as he tried to expose the wound.

"Sheriff, give me a second to try and stop the bleeding," Oli hissed.

Using the good knife, he cut pieces off the sheriff's shirt tail and fashioned a quick bandage. While doing so, he listened for footsteps from the robbers. By this time they would have their rifles reloaded.

"Get me my Hawken," Tomson said.

"It's on your horse and it run back down the road," Oli told him.

He helped the sheriff sit up. The wounded man was sweating and his face was pale. Oli had heard of this happening to someone who was injured. He needed to get the man back lying down.

"I'll go get the robbers, Ben," he said. "You're going to be in trouble if you keep sitting up."

The sheriff began to shake and Oli laid him back down. He pulled Tomson's Colt from its holster and put it in his hand. "If you see anyone but me come this way, send a few bullets his way."

Crouching next to the outcrop, Oli took the boots off. They were a bit loose on his feet and he couldn't afford to have a misstep getting over the rocks above the robbers. He could hear the sheriff's mustang coming back.

Again a rifle sounded, the bullet striking the cantle of the saddle. The horse squatted and leaped forward, running to the west. At the same moment, Oli sprinted across the road gaining protection behind the sandstone cliff on the other side.

The surprise from his move prevented Rex or Harry from getting a shot at him. Oli hesitated only a second before starting to work his way up the cliff. He could hear swearing coming from the direction of the robbers.

Digging his fingers and toes into the cracks in the rock he climbed, looking up, his heart hammering in his chest. At any moment he expected one of the men to come out and find him helpless on the wall. He wanted to look back toward the sheriff, but didn't dare to take the focus off his climb.

He could see the blood on his fingers that were being torn by the rough stone and knew by the feel that his feet were in the same shape. The months of wandering in the wilderness had left Oli thin, but the muscles were toned.

Crawling over the edge of the 30 foot high cliff, he lay on his back, sucking air into his burning lungs and waiting for the ache to leave his legs and arms. Checking his knife and Colt, then moving soundlessly across the flat top of the sandstone cliff while keeping low, he approached the far edge.

He heard the voices of the robbers. One of them wanted to cut and run, while the other worried about riding away out in the open and being shot. The sun had come out and it was hot on the rock. Sweat was running down Oli's forehead and burning his eyes.

He worked his way to the edge and peered over. He could see Harry lying over a boulder with his rifle at the ready. Rex was out of sight. The men were about 150 feet away, within the range of the Colt, but the .28 caliber might not be a killing shot.

Oli knew that once they knew he was up here, one man could keep him pinned on top while the other worked his way around, possibly even finishing off the sheriff. To his left were a series of boulders that would allow him to climb down and get behind the men. Once down, he would be out of range for the Colt. He would have to work his way in closer.

Knowing that he could do little good from the top, he moved back from the edge and went to the boulders. His left big toe was throbbing and he looked down. The nail was half torn off. He shuddered and pushed it to the back of his mind. There was nothing he could do about it right now.

Climbing down through the boulders, he made sure that the gun didn't scrape or hit against the rock, giving away his presences. All of a sudden, he froze. Just below him were the robbers' horses. They would whinny, snort, or stomp when they noticed him.

He was unable to see Harry or Rex behind the rocks near the road. Knowing that he had no choice, Oli continued down, getting closer to the animals.

He knew that they had caught his scent because they began to get restless.

He made sure that the loop was off the Colt. It was loaded with four bullets, with the hammer on an empty chamber. In the possible bag he had an additional loaded cylinder. He would have to remove the barrel to put the loaded cylinder on the spindle. If it came to needing it, he hoped that he would have good cover for the time it would take.

Oli was about to step out from behind a boulder, exposing himself to the horses, when there was the sound of running footsteps. Suddenly, Rex was only ten paces from him. Both men saw each other at the same time.

"What the . . ." Rex uttered and swung his rifle in Oli's direction. Hearing the footsteps before seeing the robber had warned him, and Oli already had the Colt out if its holster. The revolver bucked in his hand, the bullet striking Rex in the chest.

In a reflex motion, the robber pulled the trigger and the bullet struck the boulder next to Oli, sending shards of rock cutting into his leg. Rex went to his knees, dropping the rifle, clawing at his revolver.

Oli squeezed the trigger again, hitting the man just below the eye. Rex collapsed backwards, his legs twisted under him. The startled horses pulled their pickets loose and were running east toward the river.

"Rex! Hey, Rex!" Harry shouted. "Did you get him?"

There was the sound of metal on rock as Harry worked his way back toward the horses. He then saw the animals, standing with their heads up, looking back toward the boulders.

"Damn it! Is that you rag man?" he shouted. "I should have killed you when I saw you in the cell."

"Drop your guns and step out with your hands up, and I'll let you live," Oli called back to the robber. "Your partner back here didn't get the same chance."

He heard Harry running and braced himself for the confrontation. Then he realized that the steps were going away. He was after one of the mustangs! There was a good chance that the sheriff would be unable to defend himself and would be killed.

Oli scooped up the extra revolver from Rex and ran after the fleeing man. He caught a glimpse of Harry's coattail as he went behind a large rock ahead of him. Oli knew that the robber could stop and wait for him to come out into the open, then shoot him, but hoped that he would continue after a horse.

As he rounded the boulder on the road, his worst fear was realized. Harry stood in the road with his rifle up, waiting. There was a shot and Oli threw himself to the ground, trying to avoid being hit.

Rolling to his side, he brought up the Colt just in time to see Harry fall full-length into the dust of the road. Behind him, Sheriff Tomson stood holding his smoking Hawken. The sheriff lowered the rifle and leaned heavily against the sandstone boulders.

Breathing heavily, Tomson called out, "Damn you, August! You don't just run into the open when chasing a man!"

Shaking from the close call, Oli replied, "I'll try and remember that."

There was no doubt that luck had been with Oli this day. The mustang had come back to the sheriff and he had been able to get his rifle. He had then been waiting, in case Oli was able to flush out the robbers.

After making sure that the sheriff's wound hadn't started bleeding again, he then went and checked the two robbers for the money belt or gold. Neither had it on them. He then got the mustang and went after the robbers' horses.

The skittish animals kept their distance as he tried to get close. "You stubborn cusses better sit still. Don't make me shoot you to check them saddle bags," he threatened.

After a lot of work he was able to herd the animals back to the sandstone outcrop. The mustang that he was riding was a fair cutting horse. It almost unseated him as it prevented the robbers' horses from getting around them. After getting his hands on the picket ropes, he checked the saddle bags and bed rolls. Again, he found nothing.

He walked back to the sheriff. "Could they have hidden it along the way and planned to come back?" Oli asked.

"Not these boys," Tomson replied. "They didn't trust anyone, much less each other. If I had to guess, it will be near where they were waiting for us."

Oli walked toward the spot, his stomach tight with fear that they wouldn't find the gold. He spotted the men's possible bags between two rocks. He emptied them without success. He continued to check around the area muttering and swearing to himself.

Finally, he caught sight of something in a split in the wall. The money belt lay with a powder horn, some lead balls and oiled patches. He opened the money belt and looked at the gold coins. Relief flooded over him. Unbuttoning his shirt, he put the belt around his waist. The familiar weight put a broad smile on his face.

CHAPTER FIFTEEN

They were only four hours from Dubuque and the sheriff had a ball in his chest. Tomson insisted that he would be able to ride. The shock of being hit had subsided. Oli loaded the two robbers onto their horses, tying their hands and feet together under the animals' bellies.

While doing so, he began to shake. The sheriff, watching this, said, "You best sit down, son. You are white as a ghost."

The realization that he had killed a man and almost gotten killed himself suddenly hit him. All the adrenalin and the urgency to find the gold had carried him this far, but suddenly it wasn't enough.

"I . . . I guess, I hadn't thought about having to kill someone," he said, breathing deep to try to settle himself down.

"It was the only option these men gave us. It was kill or be killed," the sheriff said.

"Sheriff Tomson," Oli said, "was the gold worth taking the lives of these men?"

"Son, do you think I came after these men just because of the gold you lost?" Tomson asked. "Your gold and what you do with it don't mean spit to me. I come because of the young man laying with his head split open back in Pony Hollow, and for all the others they had done injustice to."

"Don't get me wrong. It wasn't right when I put you in jail. My believing the Wolfes and then blabbing about the gold is what caused all of this, and I will have to live with it. Mr. August, I would like to believe it was more than the gold that brought you with me after these men. I want you to know, I appreciated you dragging me out of the road and am proud of the way you handled yourself."

Oli helped the sheriff onto his horse and then climbed onto the other mustang with the robbers' horses in tow. The sheriff's words kept going through his mind. He thought about what had been on his mind since leaving Pony Hollow. Had it just been getting the gold back? To make sure that the trip to the Rockies hadn't been for nothing? Then a smile came to his face. He was thinking about Joan. The gold was not to buy her love, but for their future should she have him.

The two men spent three days in Dubuque. The doctor got the ball out of the sheriff's chest. It had stopped shy of the lung and had chipped a couple of ribs. He would be out of action for a month.

The marshal in Dubuque had posters on the robbers. Each had a $500 reward on them. Sheriff Tomson insisted that Oli take it. Arrangements were made for a buckboard to ride back to Pony Hollow. Oli was able to keep Harry's and Rex's horses and gear. What money that they'd had in their pockets was used to bury the men.

No mention had been made about the gold that Oli carried around his waist. They didn't need any other lowlifes coming after them. During the ride back, Tomson brought up the problem that both he and the deputy were injured.

"I need another deputy. Chet and I are both out for a while. It would be a great help if you would do this for me."

"I don't know anything about being a lawman," Oli objected.

"You know more than you think, Oli. All I'm asking is that you show the badge around town."

"I'm not sure if I'll be staying," Oli said, delaying any decision. "I'll let you know after we get back."

Eight days after they rode out of Pony Hollow they arrived back in town. Oli drove the buckboard straight to the doc's. After helping Sheriff Tomson into the office, he took the buckboard and the horses to the livery. Thanking the hostler, he then brought Joan's father's horse to their house.

Joan met him at the door, her eyes shining. "Chet is awake. He doesn't remember a thing about the attack, but other than that he's doing okay."

"That is wonderful news," Oli replied. "I brought your father's horse back. I'll take it to your barn and give it a good rubdown before I leave."

"Oli, when you finish with the horse, you come back here and join us for supper," she insisted.

There was nothing that he would have liked more, but he was in need of a bath and still hadn't gotten a shave and haircut. He didn't want her parents to see him looking this way. He had planned his next visit to be after he'd made himself presentable.

"I would not be very good company the way I look," he said. "I'll be back after I have a chance to clean up a bit."

"Supper is in a half-hour. There is a basin and water near the back door. I am expecting you to be here," she said and, flipping her hair, Joan walked to the kitchen.

The supper was very good. There was a beef roast, new potatoes, carrots, and cold milk. Everyone was anxious to hear about catching the robbers. Oli had done his best to clean up before the meal, but he knew that he was pretty rough looking.

After the meal was over, he had a short visit with the deputy. Chet was having some trouble with double vision, but each day it was getting better. He left Joan's house and figured that he would see if he could sleep in the livery.

He noticed a light in the doctor's office. Tapping on the door, he heard a grunt that he assumed was an invitation to enter. A low lamp was burning in the front of the room. Lying on a cot in the back was Sheriff Tomson.

He tried to sit up a little when Oli entered, but the pain of his wound was too much and he slumped back down on the bed.

"I didn't mean to wake you, sheriff," he apologized.

"I wasn't sleeping, Oli," Tomson told him. "The damn bandage is too tight and making the ribs hurt."

"I was heading for the livery when I saw the light."

"You weren't going to sleep in the livery, were you?" the sheriff asked.

"It's late and I will look for a room to rent tomorrow," Oli told him.

"I want you to stay on the cot in the jail tonight," Tomson said. "Have you decided about the deputy job?"

Thinking of the smile that Joan had given him, Oli replied, "I have decided to stay around for a while. I would be looking for work and the deputy job would solve that."

The sheriff had Oli raise his hand as he swore him in. "I got badges in the desk drawer. Put it on when you're making rounds. The pay is $45 a month."

It was dark and Oli sat in the brick and stone building with the lantern low. He was enjoying a mug of coffee and cleaning the Colt. He wasn't anxious to turn in. He had been having dreams that Rex was coming at him and his gun wouldn't fire. He would wake up sweating, unable to get back to sleep.

He had found his ledger lying on the desk when he got back. Finding a pencil in the desk, he began to list his assets. The gold, the rewards, the horses, their gear. He stopped and wrote in the page, "too many to count".

Two weeks ago he was wandering in the woods. A week ago he was a prisoner and the gold was gone. Now he had that and more. He was even running the jail. He sat for a while, thinking about Joan before lying on the cot.

"Damn," he said. "I think the bunks in the cell are more comfortable that his cot." Oli was up before daylight. He started a list of things he had to do:

Bring the gold to the bank.
Telegram to Don Sikes family.
New set of clothes, hat, boots.
Bath, haircut, shave.
Colt and holster, possible bag.
See about property.
Axe, broad axe, auger, saw, hammer.
Make rounds around town.

He pondered the list, knowing that there were many more things. He added to the list flint and steel. It was getting light outside. He went to the outhouse and then stopped at the mirror and ran his fingers through his hair. He looked at the hat that he had gotten from Joan. It was a fine hat. He would look for another like it.

Joan was working at the café when he got there for breakfast. She smiled and chatted with the customers as she got them their food, spending a little extra time at his table. He had seen the house her folks had, and the barns and yards. He was sure that she didn't have to work if she didn't want to. Many young women her age were sent to school in the east.

Leaving some money for his meal on the table, he turned to leave. "We'll have raspberry pie with supper tonight. I hope you can join us," she called to him.

Oli's first stop was at the telegraph office. He sent a short note to Philadelphia, hoping it would get to the family of Don Sikes. It said far too little of what he felt inside. His next stop was the bank.

The man at the bank took a hard look at Oli when he walked in. The heavy iron safe in the back looked like it could keep the likes of Rex and Harry out. The man's attitude changed quickly when Oli took the coins out and laid them on the desk.

The plan was to find someone in the market for old Spanish coins. It could bring in more than the value of the gold, which was already considerable. Oli had kept back some coins to look at and touch every so often.

He used one of the coins at the mercantile when the owner, George Walters, had looked down his nose when Oli had placed the order for new clothes and other items. When the Spanish coin landed on his counter, his look became much more pleasant. Most things that he needed he planned to pay for with the reward money.

The barber, Ralph also offered bathes. He took his time soaking in the warm water. He scrubbed the dirt out of his calloused hands. He had lost two toenails from climbing the cliff. There was much discussion of how he wanted his hair and if he should keep a moustache. He left with his hair cut just above the ear and a full moustache on his upper lip.

Leaving the barber's, he wore his new clothing. The wool shirt and pants were summer weight and were blue, much like the ones he had gotten from Joan. The boots he'd bought had a square toe and low heel. They came up just above the ankle.

He bought one of the latest Colt Paterson revolvers, with the loading lever built in. The possible bag was filled with almost everything that he would need. He then dropped the borrowed clothing at a woman who took in washing.

His last stop was at the town land office. A balding man with a broad middle, a yellowed white shirt and a stiff collar greeted him. Oli told him about the land that he wanted to buy. Evidently, word of his spending had spread around town. The portly man shook his head and tried to convince Oli that there was a much nicer piece just east of town that would be ideal for a large home and outbuildings.

Oli stood fast and made the deal on the property that he wanted. The man promised to have the deed drawn up within the week. Finishing up at the land office, it was too late to purchase the tools that he would need to start building. Feeling good about the day, he walked over to the doc's to check on the sheriff.

Tomson was sitting in a chair at the back of the room and the doctor was changing his bandage. "Damn! Look at you," he said, smiling. "You clean up good, and the badge looks right at home. Is that one of them new Colts you got on your side?"

"It is, and I got a Hawken .50 ordered. Walters says it should be in from St. Louis in a week or two," Oli replied.

"Do you think you'll have to fight a war here in Pony Hollow?" the sheriff kidded him.

"If I do, I'll be ready," Oli replied, giving it back to the sheriff.

He was glad to see that the sheriff was feeling better. Leaving the doctor's, he stopped by the office and dropped off the new Colt before going to supper. If Oli thought that he'd felt uncomfortable in the dirty clothing yesterday, he felt even more awkward in the new store bought clothing at supper that night. He wasn't sure what the looks that he was getting from everyone meant, but at least they weren't ones of distaste.

The deputy joined them for the meal. He was wearing a patch over one eye to help with the double vision. Joan was busy helping her mother serve the meal. Her father asked him about the horses he had brought back. Oli told him that he planned to ride the bay gelding and possibly trade or sell the other.

With the meal done, Joan joined him on the front porch. "You looked a little stiff at supper tonight," she mentioned.

"I think it was the clothing," he explained. "The new stuff is awful hard to break in."

"The lady in town brought Martin's clothes back today," she said.

They continued making small talk for a while until Joan's mother called her in to help. Oli thanked her for supper and headed for the jail. He muttered to himself as he walked back, wishing that he was smoother talking to women. Just before reaching the brick and stone building, Tate Wolfe stepped out in front of him.

"Little man, you best stay away from Joan Maier," he threatened Oli.

Oli looked up at the scowling face. "What, and who, I visit is my business," he snapped.

"My brother and I run things here in Pony Hollow, and by damn we can run you out of town," the bold man warned.

"Mr. Wolfe. There are a few things you should consider. I am the law in Pony Hollow right now. I like Joan Maier and plan to continue seeing her, and while I may appear to be unarmed, giving you courage . . ." Then, with a swift motion, Oli drew the good knife, throwing it into the post next to Tate.

Wide-eyed, the man looked at the knife. "I am always armed," Oli warned.

Stepping onto the porch of the jail, he pulled the knife and put it back into the sheath. Then Oli turned to the big man. "I understand you and your brother run a freight line and handle lumber. I will be coming to see you in the next couple of days to talk about ordering some."

Leaving the speechless Tate Wolfe standing in the street, Oli went into the jail and checked the coffee pot. His hand was shaking just a bit.

For the next two weeks Oli kept busy between showing the badge in Pony Hollow and starting to build a small house on the property he had bought. While the Wolfes had no use for him, they were still willing to sell him the boards he needed.

He had breakfast every morning at the café. Joan would brighten his day with her smile. She invited him to a picnic after church on Sunday. Oli had expanded his wardrobe to include a dark wool suit and a broad brimmed, crowned hat. While the suit was hot and tended to be itchy, it was proper for social gatherings.

It was late summer, and Oli was shingling the roof of the two-room building on his property. The sun was hot and he was working with his shirt off, sweat glistening on his lean body.

"Are you going to make this building your life's work?" Joan called to him. "I have been watching you. It will be snowing before you get done."

Scrambling down the ladder, Oli blushed as he pulled on his shirt. "I apologize, Miss Maier. Had I known you were coming out, I would have been properly dressed."

She shaded her eyes and looked out at the Turkey River. "I have always loved this place."

"You told me that the day we met," Oli said. Staring at his shoes and kicking the dust, he mumbled, "That's why I bought it for you."

"Excuse me," Joan said. "I missed what you said."

His blue eyes looked into her hazel ones. Suddenly his mouth was dry and he sorely wished that he had a drink of water. "I . . ." he started, then his voice became stronger. "I bought this land for you."

"For me?" she said. "Why for me?"

Damn, he thought, *she isn't making this easy.*

"You loved this spot, and . . . and I have loved you since the first time I saw you." Once said, Oli's whole body was tingling with anticipation.

Looking back at the river, she said, "Oh. I thought it was my cooking that brought you around."

Oli didn't trust his tongue. He knew that he would only blather if he tried to talk. The two of them watched two ducks on the river for a moment. He no longer felt the sun, heard the birds or the breeze in the trees. He ached inside to hear any acknowledgement that she felt the same way.

"Well," she finally said, "we have problem."

"What problem?" he asked, fearing the answer.

"Oli August," she began, "I have felt the same way you do, since we first met. But loving you isn't enough for us to marry."

"You would marry me?" he asked.

"Of course I would, but it would have to be with the blessing of my father," she explained.

Moving close to Joan, he put his arm around her and they stood unaware of anything but each other.

Suddenly, Joan asked, "Would this be our house?"

Smiling, Oli took her hand and led her inside, "It is small, but I thought it would be enough to start."

She walked through the small two-room home, pointing out all the things that she would like to do to the inside. He assured her that this house was just a start and that he had plans for a log home above the river, so they could sit and watch the sunset every evening.

Suddenly, she exclaimed, "I got to get back to work!" As she ran out the door, Joan called back, "Come to supper tonight. You can ask my father."

Little got done the rest of the day. Every time Oli tried to start something, his mind was elsewhere and the project was forgotten. Finally, he bathed and dressed in his Sunday suit. He was early for supper, but could not put off talking to her father any longer.

He knocked on the door and heard someone call, "Come in."

He found the ladies cooking in the kitchen. Joan met him, wiping the flour off her hands. Her mother busied herself, and had a broad smile on her face. Joan took his hand. "Father is in the barn. It will be two hours before supper."

"I'll go and see him," Oli said. Leaving by the back door, he headed for the barn. Mr. Maier had just started cleaning the stalls. He looked up and acknowledged Oli as he entered.

Working to getting his courage up to ask him, Oli removed his coat, grabbed a fork and started helping. Her father made small talk of how hot it had been and about how the garden was doing.

After the barn was cleaned and the animals fed, her father asked him if he would like to see the garden. The two men stood looking at the tomatoes and other vegetables. Oli had his coat hanging over his arm and was trying to wipe the manure off his boots.

"Mr. Maier," he started. "I have been seeing your daughter for a while and we have grown close."

The man looked at the nervous young man and said, "Really? I thought you come around for the meals."

Oli looked at the man, who was admiring the tomato he had picked. He was now sure that Joan had already spoken to her father. "We would like to get married, with your permission."

The father looked toward the house, his brow furled. "When we first met you, such a thought was the furthest thing from our minds. I have watched you the past couple of months and am pleased with what I've seen." Reaching out to shake Oli's hand, he said, "I would be proud to have you marry my daughter. You'll have to ask her mother at supper."

FOLLOW THE GOLD

I hope you enjoyed reading *Oli's Gold* as much as I enjoyed writing it. If you would like to continue following the gold, you can download *Search For Oli's Gold* and *Return To Oli's Gold* E Books.

My goal is to continue to provide quality books for your enjoyment. I would appreciate you taking the time to post a positive review

Watch for future books as they become available in paperback. Your support is the fuel to motivate my writing.

Best wishes and good reading.

Jim